A Novel of Shorts:

The Woman No One Sees

Leah McNaughton Lederman

Mothership Press

Sarasota, Florida

Publisher's Note: This is a work of fiction. Names, characters, places, and incidents are a product of the author's imagination. Locales and public names are sometimes used for atmospheric purposes. Any resemblance to actual people, living or dead, or to businesses, companies, events, institutions, or locales is completely coincidental.

Book Layout © 2017 BookDesignTemplates.com

A Novel of Shorts: The Woman No One Sees/ Leah McNaughton Lederman. -- 1st ed.

ISBN 978-1-948217-01-9

This book is dedicated to those with whom and for whom I have cleaned. I didn't save your dust, I promise.

CONTENTS

Foreword
By Dirk Manning

Ashes to Ashes:
A study of a mysterious stranger
always – and never – known

I have known Esther her whole life...several years...and perhaps even before she was truly born into this world from the dark recesses of the mind of author Leah Lederman.

I can't profess to fully understanding where she came from, of course, and were I to press the issue – which I won't – I'm not sure Leah does, either.

Esther, I suspect, just sort of wandered in from her subconscious, perhaps unassumingly pushing some dust around with her broom. I imagine she was just tidying up the place, and as such was allowed to stay...only for Leah to then realize she couldn't make her leave until it was too late.

As I imagine it, by then Esther had decorated the place with her "dust" collections – and an urn – having taken up a permanent residence without ever asking for permission...or forgiveness.

Esther now exists in Leah's mind – as she soon will yours, I suspect – in a permanent present state.

Esther was. Esther is. Esther always will be: Unassuming-yet-creepy, like that great-Aunt you never really knew who was always sitting in the back of the second room, removed, at your childhood family reunions.

As you'll see in these nine stories, Esther has a personality, of course, and is indeed a fully formed person...but I'm not sure we ever truly see her wholly, nor do I think we would ever want to.

Esther exists in the visible shadows, a three-dimensional blank slate, moving forward with a life – and I daresay a mission – that I'm not even sure she has considered the consequences of, making her equally endearing and terrifying.

I realize I'm being vague here, so let me be more explicit in what I'm trying to say before I get out of your way and let you get to enjoying the unsettling effect of these stories firsthand: In this collection (or is it a novel?) you should prepare for an discomforting and disquieting walk with a fascinating yet frustratingly mysterious and unassumingly eerie woman.

Even as I warn you of what you're about to experience, I still find myself envying you for getting to read these stories for the first time. I suspect Esther will change you, as she changed me, forever causing me to do double-takes at those visible invisibles who exist oftentimes silently on the edges of our peripheral vision while still remaining ever-present at the outskirts of our lives.

Through my experiences with Esther in this book, I now find myself reflecting on them perhaps with a little more suspicion than I should, and in doing so I am now unwillingly giving them access to my innermost mind... and perhaps that is the gift, curse, and mission of Esther.

Or maybe she's just some random weirdo with a dust fetish. Even after knowing Esther for her whole life I'm still not sure, so good luck in deciding that for yourselves, friends...

Dirk Manning is the writer of comics and graphic novels including NIGHTMARE WORLD, TALES OF MR. RHEE, LOVE STORIES (TO DIE FOR), HOPE, HAUNTED HIGH-ONS, and THE ADVENTURES OF CTHULHU JR. & DASTARDLY DIRK, many of which were edited by Leah Lederman over the years. More information about Dirk and his works can be found at www.DirkManning.com and most major social media platforms @DirkManning.

Dust to Dust

S he ran her index finger along the bookshelf, exposing the glossy cherry finish beneath it. It reflected the light from the chandelier and for a moment, she thought about the ripples in a mountain creek, eroding the mossy banks on either side. Here, the moss was a layer of gray dust, its backdrop a jagged range of leather-bound classics.

The dust was thick enough to peel from the surface like a soft, linty scab, and so she removed the bulk of it this way. Her back straightened in anticipation each time she reached another corner, and she only dared to exhale after she'd finished the peel —it was coming off in thick wallpaper strips. She'd never seen dust quite like this.

The funeral was only the day before, but clearly there had been months of neglect prior to that, time spent navigating insurance paperwork, weeping silently, packing lunches, going through the motions. And during that time, she'd sat quietly, attentively, at the bedside of someone whom, she imagined, would probably rather she went home and dusted the bookshelves.

"It will get done eventually, dear." She had said it out loud to him, there in the hospital, just to let the walls soak in something other than silence. He would not say anything. He could not. But she stayed there with him, sitting in the cold, tiled room addled with disinfectant. She put a bottle of the hospital solution in her purse one night after the nurse left. Another for her collection.

She was in his study; the dusting nearly finished. Afterwards, when she'd collected all of it, she'd try the disinfectant. The room would smell like a hospital—just the way she remembered him.

"I told you the dusting would get done," she tittered to a photograph of him on the shelf. He was on his boat, smiling at the camera. The wind made his hair stick out at a 45-degree angle like some slanted cliff. She hadn't seen his hair in a long time. The sky and water behind him were seamlessly blue, and the white spray from the boat mirrored the clouds. Her finger, grubby now from the dust, streaked slowly across the frame's glass, leaving a smooth, dusted trail behind it. A jet stream tinged with human dirt.

She returned her attention to the shelf and peeled another strip, but this one crumbled. The little scabs of dust swayed lazily to the floor, and a few particles rose up in the air around her. She paused. Were these tiny flecks like snowflakes, no two the same? Nonsense. "But they are human," she whispered to herself, "Dust is 80 percent human skin." Smiling, she began to hum a vacant tune.

This is his dust. This is him.

A blond, translucent hair poked out from the dust she'd gathered on the lower shelf and she paused, turning her head to the side while she conjured the scene that led to its placement there. She could see him, wearing the same faded shirt as the picture, smoothing his hair as if he'd just walked in from the boat ride. A single strand dwindled down across the books, undetected, as he peered absently at the leather-spined titles— the same little hair that now stuck out so obstinately from its dusty bed. His finger grazed the tops of his collection, sending tiny particles to rest on the shelf. Inhaling, he turned slowly and it seemed that he might face her. Before she could meet his eyes, though, she found herself alone in the room. Looking at the dust she'd collected, she sighed.

This is all I have, now.

When the shelves were dusted, she polished them quickly with a soft white cloth and the spray she'd taken from the hospital. It made her think of echoing footsteps and beeping machines when she breathed it in. Perhaps it is too quiet in this house, she thought silently, and began to hum softly again.

The smell followed her into the various rooms of the house, where she shoveled dust into one of the ceramic containers she carried with her, for occasions just like these, before wiping down the various surfaces. She swabbed along the tops of clocks and picture frames, behind the TV and over top of the snarled electrical cords throughout the rooms. Her empty humming tune drifted down the hall, dissipated by the hiss of the aerosol disinfectant.

She had cleaned houses before, of course, and this made things simpler—she knew the process. Once everything had been wiped clear of dust, she swept debris from the hard floors and linolcum into the only carpeted room in the house, the study. This is where she had begun. The polished shelves twinkled back at her during the few short minutes she ran the vacuum cleaner, their cleanness paralleled by the careful stripes she made along the carpet. She removed the vacuum's dirt cup and emptied its contents into her little ceramic urn, the same one that carried all of the dust strips and remnants from throughout the house.

This container was, she thought, well-chosen. There was always a small selection available in her oversized purse, and she liked that this one had a smooth stone disk for a lid. After arranging the two latches that held it in place, she wiped off the outer surface and placed the whole thing into her bag.

Once back in her own home, she carefully ran the cloth—now smudged with a gray, wrinkled handprint—across the shelf before removing the container, lid intact, from her bag and setting it carefully on the shelf between the granite jewelry box and the vintage candy tin. It was a perfect fit there, and she gave a perfunctory nod of satisfaction as she stepped back to view its spacing from the other urns. A sweet, sad little collection. Her lip had twisted upward on one end, halfway between a sob and a smirk. Indeed, it was a sweet, sad little collection…but it still needed more.

***

"Thank goodness you're here, girl! It's been a busy afternoon," Janet spoke in a hurried sigh, trying to catch her breath, "We had two new arrivals this morning and we're still trying to get things situated." A phone rang on the desk across from her. She gestured to it without looking up from the scrawled notes on her legal pad, "Do you mind grabbing that for me?"

The purse made a distinct "clink" noise as she set it down on the desk next to Janet and answered the phone, "Sheet County Hospice, how may I help you?"

The Reduction

Esther had been staring out the window for what might have been an hour. The room was clean, even down to the corners. Her mom said you could always tell how clean a place was, or how often they'd cleaned it, by how much grime was built up into the corners. Her business motto was, "We don't cut corners."

Cleaning corners was a tricky business, too—just shoving a broom or a mop against the intersection was never enough. That's how you ended up with the stubborn little dirt triangle, and the wetness of a mop would only make it sticky and let it harden into grime taffy. The trick, as always, was a little elbow grease.

Down on her hands and knees, Esther applied her old toothbrush to the final corner in her bedroom, carefully scraping the bristles outward. Even the toothbrush had its limitations. She knew she wouldn't be able to focus on anything else if she didn't clear out the gunk. It gnawed at the corners of her mind.

Elbow grease was a reliable trick but the real secret to cleaning was improvisation. You could buy every tool they advertised on TV or sold in stores, no matter how specialized, and it wouldn't win out over the toothbrush. Except today. And that's when she thought of its counterpart—the toothpick.

Her mom and sister, Johanna, were down in the kitchen prepping for the big meal, even though it was scheduled for tomorrow. There was so much to be done and, per the usual, their Mom wanted to get a head start. It wasn't often they hosted things like this, and it wasn't often that Aunt Janet's family came to visit.

Esther's cousin Bernie would be starting law school in the Fall and her mom was so proud of him that she insisted on having a big dinner when they came to town for the campus tour. Esther thought, privately, that her Mom also wanted to show Aunt Janet how fancy she could be, even if she was just a cleaning lady.

Aunt Janet had been a cleaning lady, too, even if no one liked to bring that up. Grandpa started the business with Grandma and Uncle Burt, and wrangled his children into helping out. Child labor laws be damned. Aunt Jan hated it. Esther's mom told stories of finding her sister dawdling in the parking lot, standing and staring off in the hallways, her ridiculous "hurry up and look busy" dance whenever Grandpa came loping around the corner.

Grandpa and Grandma caught on, of course. And though they tried—there were certainly some knock-down-drag-em-outs—they never were able to convince her to stay on. She refused to be stuck in mop closets with Uncle Burt, and that's all she ever said about that. She got a job at some "bougie coffeeshop," as Grandpa liked to say, and started taking courses at the community college.

Eventually Esther's Grandpa left the business to his remaining loyal daughter, Maggie, and she did the best she could with it. The woman could strip and wax a floor so that it shone like glass, could unclog any toilet, but never did manage to make heads or tails of the business aspect. Old clients died, or went out of business, or moved on, and she didn't know how to find new ones.

Before the company went belly-up, she had enough sense to sell the whole thing on the condition that they kept her on as an employee. It was a tough time, sure. Aunt Jan was outraged by the whole thing, and during the fights between the two sisters, Esther and Johanna learned a lot of new curse words.

Esther picked the last bit of dirt away from the corner with the toothpick, its pointed end now stubby from being jammed into the corner too many times. She brushed the tiny granules onto a sheet of paper and used it to funnel the tiny particles into a clear glass bottle. When she was finished, she set the bottle in its place in her closet.

She'd never understood why Aunt Janet was so angry about the cleaning business. Things got funny around death, is what her mom had said. There was never a way to predict the ways grief would rear its ugly head. For some people it was the money, of course. But then it could be a set of golf clubs, a stamp collection, a photo frame. Or a business. In this case, it seemed Aunt Janet really just wanted to watch the whole thing burn to the ground.

That was all years ago. The sisters had forgiven each other, like sisters do, or at least moved past it, like sisters do. And even if Esther's mom and aunt didn't see each other often, when they spoke on the phone the house filled with Maggie's barking laugh. Esther would sit on the steps and listen, waiting to hear a juicy bit about Bernie and his little sister Francie, or even better, a little tidbit about herself or Johanna.

That's how Esther knew her mom wanted Johanna to go to college. "Johanna needs something more than I can give her, and I don't where else she'd get it than by sitting in one of those fancy lecture halls." Her mother paused, listening to Aunt Janet's input, then replied. "Esther can just stay here a little while longer. She's the best helper with the business."

Maggie still referred to it as the business, even if it wasn't technically hers. Talking about it like that seemed a smart way to avoid thinking about the horrible arguments they'd had. Esther was glad her mother wanted her, though something prickled at the back of her heart like a worry or a hurt. Was college better? Was Johanna better?

Esther had thrown herself into their cleaning nights. She scrubbed floorboards and stood on stools to reach cobwebs. She nodded, mentally taking notes as her mother reviewed her work, the older woman squeaking clean an errant fingerprint along the way. She'd point at the offending fuzz or streak without saying a word and Esther followed on her heels, cleaning caddy at the ready.

Once Esther had put away her little glass bottle of sand, as she called it, and looked around the room for anything else to tidy. Johanna was right—Mom was definitely getting a little nervous about the whole ordeal. It created an underlying, unidentifiable tension in the air. The prime objective was to stay out of sight, but if you were in range, you'd better be working. After she'd changed out the garbage can again, she sat looking about with her hands in lap, wondering what to do next. Esther felt safe for the time being, as her Mom was busy downstairs on the phone, probably making last minute plans with Aunt Jan.

Johanna had opted to help with the cooking. She had a natural sense for it, and even seemed to enjoy it. Often, Esther watched her mother and sister sitting there at the table simply talking about the process of cooking. It boggled her. Hadn't they just prepared the meal, minutes before? It was like sports commentators between quarters, regurgitating the game points they'd just watched play out.

Johanna came into their shared room then, settling onto the bed with a dramatic sigh. "I can't wait till this is all over with and we can go back to not pretending we're hoity-toities. I really just want mac and cheese for dinner."

"Lasagna's good," Esther said with a shrug. "I can't remember the last time Mom made it."

Johanna paged through a magazine. "Yeah, I think plans just changed."

Esther stopped admiring the non-existent corner grime. "Oh?"

Johanna peered at the magazine's pages with rapt interest. She loved holding information over her sister. She feigned surprise when she looked up and saw Esther waiting. "Mom didn't seem happy when she got off the phone. Sounds like Jan's got other plans." She said this last in a sort of ominous sing-song.

Esther digested this for a moment before asking, softly, "How's Mom…doing?"

"She just went to bed. Lights off in ten minutes, she said."

The clock said ten pm. Normally their mother didn't care how late the girls stayed up, but if she said lights out, they both knew there was trouble. Having made her dramatic announcement, Johanna joined Esther in quietly preparing for bed. Both of them were sure to insert the discarded clothes in the hamper. *Maybe Mom will sleep it off*, Esther thought to herself, hoping herself to sleep that there wouldn't be an explosion.

***

"Bernie wants steak at his celebratory dinner, and what can I say? The men in this family do love a good steak. Your dad did, that's for sure."

At these words, Esther looked up from her cereal. She looked over at Johanna, who was also paying close attention. Their mother rarely mentioned their father.

"And he knows best how to work the grill, Aunt Jan says." Maggie put some dishes in the sink, with a bit more force than was necessary. "Still, I think Johanna and I can whip up Grandma's bearnaise sauce. It will be a good time." Johanna's head nearly fell off from nodding it so hard.

Esther was relieved to spend the afternoon visit playing checkers in the living room with her cousin Francie. She listened while her mom, sister, and Aunt Janet sang Loretta Lynn in the kitchen, and cast an occasional glance at their gathering through the archway. It was a cloying moment, the three women so aware of "making memories" that they were manufacturing them instead. Bernie stood sulking by the grill on the back porch, smoking cigarettes and ignoring the women.

They'd just finished "Coal Miner's Daughter" and Aunt Jan laughed, wiping her eyes with her sleeve. "I used to love singing that with Dad. Remember?"

"On that old twelve-string." Esther's Mom finished off her glass of wine, settling into the memory. "Hey Esther!" she called, as if remembering she had another daughter. "What do you say? Can I show you a few chords?"

Esther frowned. "You already did, Mom!" The faux-sentimentality of the moment was lost on her. She liked memories she could feel, touch. Handle.

The women in the kitchen had already moved on without her. "Esther's got great guitar hands, Jan, you should see—"

Aunt Jan interrupted, "Oh, that reminds me! Francie's just finished learning 'Claire de Lune.'" You'd think it was the CD playing, not a twelve-year-old."

"*Mmm hmm.*" Esther heard her mother pour another glass of wine.

Esther stiffened. A room away, she instinctively knew Johanna had done the same.

In the face of any affront, perceived or otherwise, their mother had a way of stopping short and retreating beyond words. She was still restraining herself, though. Esther figured that enough planning had gone into this weekend her mother would only put forth her best behavior. Still, the two girls took this simple humming sound as a signal to tread lightly. Esther looked around at the corners of the room and wondered idly if she should start a load of laundry.

Bernie banged in from the back deck. "Steaks still saucing up, Aunt Maggie?" He pulled off his jacket and tossed it over the chair. It slipped and fell to the floor.

Esther heard her mother's low "Mm hmm" over the sound of even more wine pouring and set to straightening things in the living room, fluffing pillows and straightening the armrests on the couch.

Bernie came into the den and sat down, squishing the pillows around him. He stunk like cigarettes. Esther jumped when he hollered back to the kitchen. "Grandma's bearnaise, eh, Johanna? You're learning from the best in the business."

He sniffed a few times and wiped his nose, then sat forward and poked his little sister between the shoulder blades. "Aw, c'mon, Francie. Tell me you didn't let Esther win again! She's gotta learn sometime." He rubbed his nose again. Esther shuddered.

"Hey Bernie," Aunt Janet said, walking into the room. She called back over her shoulder to the kitchen. "Keep whisking, Jo. Don't stop whatever you do." Turning back to her son, she asked, "You still have Grandpa's twelve-string? I think you ended up with it after everything, right?

Bernie was looking around the room for the remote. "Uh, yeah, Ma. I dunno. It was in Eric's basement when he got all that flooding."

"Too bad," Aunt Janet shrugged and headed back to the kitchen.

Esther heard the clinking sound of her mom's wine glass on the counter, and she heard Johanna double up on the whisking. "You need to get the stuff off the sides, Jo," her mother said. "Don't let it get all lumpy."

Aunt Jan leaned in to inspect the contents of the bowl. "Oh yeah, that looks great. Set that down right in here, and now let's go check out the tarragon." She moved past her sister to open the fridge. Maggie took a step back and watched for a few moments as her daughter and sister bent over the mixing bowl, then exited the kitchen.

"Bernie," she said, her voice thinly bladed. Esther saw the edges of her mouth were set. "If you want to throw the steaks on, I think everything else will be ready by the time they've finished in there."

Bernie was staring at the game on the television and didn't look at his aunt when she spoke. He slapped his thigh and bellowed "OHH! The quarterback is *killing* it!" He threw himself back into the couch and thumbed at his nose. "What's that, Aunt Mags? Uh, yeah. I'll get those steaks on in a minute. Oh crap! You know what, Est? I think I forgot to turn the grill on." He leaned forward while he flipped through more channels.

"It's your turn, Esther!" Francie announced, beaming at the board. Her win was inevitable. Esther gave a smile and tried to study the squares, but her attention was on her mother, walking out of the room and out the back door. Esther was mildly annoyed at being assigned grill duty, but acutely alarmed at a possible delay in the meal. Things needed to run on schedule; she had to get that grill going. After plunking one of her checkers onto the next square, she hurried out of the room.

Maggie was already back in the kitchen, rooting around in the fridge and setting things down on the counter with deliberate thunks. *Bernie.* Esther prayed silently. *Get out there and get to work.* She was putting on her jacket when her mother's voice stopped her.

"No need to rush, Esther. I got the grill going." She was standing with her back to the counter, resting her elbows on it and taking a deep sip of wine.

Esther nodded and started to put her jacket back on the chair, but caught her mother watching her over the rim of her glass. Esther stepped to the hall closet, deftly grabbing Bernie's coat, too. Her heart was racing. She cast a look at her sister and saw that the muscles in Johanna's neck were taut. She was nodding tersely while Aunt Jan talked about tarragon or some spice, but Esther knew Johanna was picking up on the climate in the room, too.

She had swept the floor before their guests arrived, and the table was already cleared, but after Esther had hung up both coats, she studied the room for anything else she could do look busy. It was never wise to be idle when her mother started humming. Sometimes it helped assuage the mood if Maggie saw her daughters cleaning. When the tension was climbing, it was best to clear away anything that might shatter—or hurt—when hurled across the room.

Dishes. There they were, unwashed and glaring at Esther from the sink. With an inward sigh of relief at the prospect of a task, she rolled up her sleeves and started tossing silverware into the dishwasher. There were a few coffee mugs, and a bowl of some sort of pudding that looked like it could use a rinse.

The gleaming stainless-steel bowl, unmarred by the presence of soiled cutlery or lipsticked-mugs, was somehow a comfort. A distorted mirror; a receptacle. She gave it a quick wipe with the sponge before stepping out of the way. Johanna and Aunt Jan were rushing around her, cooking and pouring and stirring, and her mother was fingering the stem of her wine glass. Esther knew she needed to stay out of the way, make herself scarce. But she'd done her small part, even if no one else noticed.

Stepping away from the sink, she decided that setting the table could also be a help. Bearnaise sauce and conversation weren't her strong points, but she could set a table. Her lips moved silently as she counted plates, placing forks and knives neatly beside them. She nearly bumped into Johanna, carrying a tray filled with freshly-chopped tarragon. Its scent twirled through the air as the sisters sidestepped each other, swerving slightly and carrying on in their tasks. A well-oiled machine.

Except that Esther didn't anticipate her sister's sudden pause, or the question at the end of it.

"Has anyone seen the béarnaise?"

The room stopped. Maggie looked up from her wine; Aunt Jan stalked over to examine the empty sink. "Who…?"

She didn't have to finish the sentence. Simultaneously, she and Johanna turned over their shoulders and looked at Esther. Standing side by side with shoulders turned, it was like they parted the Red Sea between them.

Esther felt her face growing hot as dread washed over her, the old familiar sense of fear climbing her body alongside their accusing, questioning eyes, tightening her skin and curling her fingers. No one spoke a word. No one had to.

"Tell me you didn't, Esther." Johanna's voice was half reproach, half earnest plea.

Esther's breath caught in her throat as desperate thoughts rolled out in her head like ticker tape. "I—I…" The words wound themselves around Esther's tongue until they formed into the most pathetic admission, the story of her life: "I was just trying to help."

The forks in her hand clattered to the floor but she didn't stop to pick them up. She was running, running up the stairs, tripping as she neared the landing, brushing tears of shame from her face until she reached her bed and buried them deep into her pillow.

Downstairs, Esther heard the voices of her aunt and sister grow shrill, countered by her mother's smoky baritone. They grew louder until the slow stomping of feet indicated that Bernie had left the couch. His voice mixed with the womens', intoning curiously and with an amused hinge. She couldn't hear their words, just Charlie-Brown murmurs, and then Bernie was laughing loudly, cruelly, even, and his footsteps were coming up the stairs, along with his sniffling nose.

Esther lurched from the bed and scanned the room wildly. She couldn't let him find her. She hunkered down and slid her thin frame underneath the bed, snaking behind shoes and unlabeled boxes, covering parts of herself with a few discarded shirts that had made their way to the netherworld beneath the bed.

She held her breath when Bernie slammed the door open and then ambled in. She sensed his eyes taking in the room, sniffing about like a ringwraith. "Esther, seriously?" He let out a mocking laugh. "What did you do this time? How can someone be so retarded?"

His feet stopped in front of the bed, the worker boots' toes staring right at Esther. And then there were his eyes, when he knelt down and peeked beneath the bed. "Esther, this whole thing might be funny if you're weren't acting like a such a freak. Hiding under the bed? How old are you?"

His fat, hairy fingers pulled a box out of the way and Esther yelped.

"C'mon, really? What are you afraid of? Mommy gonna get you with the belt?" His eyes grew hard and he yanked a few more things out from under the bed. Esther flattened herself against the wall as best she could, but his fingers swiped toward her until he managed to grab hold of a chunk of her hair. "C'mon, Esther. I don't want it to be like this."

Esther winced and grabbed his hands to lessen the sting on her scalp. "Just leave me alone, Bernie. Why are you even here?"

"Because it's time to eat dinner, even without that stupid special sauce you ruined, you idiot. I don't know what the hell you're doing, but it's starting to piss me off. Get your ass out from under that bed!" He squeezed her hair more firmly and started to pull her toward him.

Esther hit at his arms with her free hand, and used her legs to brace herself like a cat holding itself back from water. Her cousin threw himself onto his stomach and somehow fit his other arm underneath the bed, grabbing hold of her wrists. She flailed, mute and horrible, her lips tucked tight beneath her teeth until she tasted blood. Her whole body thrashed, a silent pantomime of terror.

Bernie let go and pushed himself to his knees, panting. "You are a fucking retard, Esther. Something is seriously wrong with you. When you get over yourself and out of your psychosis, you need to get your scrawny ass down the stairs to let everyone know you're sorry. Because you are sorry, aren't you?" His feet thudded toward the stairway, muttering. "Fucking reject."

Esther counted backward from five hundred, waiting for her heart to slow down, her breathing measured. She rubbed her sore scalp where Bernie had yanked on her hair, then pressed an ear to the floor and listened to the blurred voices below. Here and there was a flute of laughter. Maybe she hadn't ruined everything. The thought was enough to draw her out from beneath the bed.

She straightened the covers on the bed and then straightened herself before the mirror. Her eyes were puffy and her hair a mess. She dragged her fingers through her hair, though more gently than Bernie had done, and looked over at the hook her dad had installed for her childhood "spider broom." It was long gone, just like he was.

"I can do this," she muttered to herself.

Their house had never been a great one for sneaking, though Esther knew the best places to set her weight down on each step. Bernie had the game on loud enough that no one noticed her slinking down the stairs. She listened to the light conversation taking place between her mother, aunt, and sister. Francie had joined them, too. They were all laughing.

"Oh yeah, I remember that day!" Esther's mother was talking easily with her sister and daughter, all trace of menace gone from her voice. "Didn't you trip over your own bookbag on your way to hug grandma?"

Aunt Jan and Johanna laughed along with her. It was just a normal evening. A normal situation, women talking together around a table, a detestable man watching the game too loud in the next room. Esther exhaled, steeling herself. She could sit down and eat. It would be like nothing had happened.

Her mother's voice ringing out over the laughter. "Well, at least you didn't have to run upstairs and hide under the bed for an hour."

The women laughed even harder. The sound of it slammed against Esther, pinning her to the wall. She struggled to breathe through her humiliation as she made her way back up the stairs, though not as quietly this time.

She stopped on the landing and, not knowing what else to do with herself, sat down next to the basket of clean clothes and began to fold them, sobbing wretchedly. She laid out each shirt across her legs, checking that the seams were straight. Wiping her eyes and cursing with indignation, she creased the edges each time she made a fold. The smoothness of the motion soothed her. By the third shirt, she had quieted herself.

With controlled movements, she placed each item back into the basket according to its category: shirt, shirt, pants, socks… She had made up her mind. She walked through the rooms, placing each crisp pile on the appropriate bed. Folded clothes. Something to remember her by.

On the way out of her mother's room, she put down the clothesbasket and reached into the closet. There in the closet, right on the shelf where it had sat since its initial placement, she felt the cardboard box.

Esther added the box to her own pile of folded clothes in the suitcase on her bed, then tossed in some toiletries and a new toothbrush—she'd ruined hers on the grimy corner while cleaning the night before. She placed the jewelry box her grandmother had given her in one of the inner pockets, along with her glass bottles. Everything she needed was there, tucked away; everything in its place.

No, something was missing. After studying the contents of her suitcase for a few moments, she took out one of the bottles. This one was empty. She turned to the wall and unscrewed the spider broom hook. Using her finger, she carefully wiped the thread of the screw clean of drywall plaster, and then scraped her finger clean on the lip of the glass bottle she'd retrieved from the case. Tiny little particles flecked from her fingers and joined the other dust.

Now she was ready to leave.

Sweep It Under the Rug

Esther fell into his knee, gladly, and squeezed. Daddy was home.

He had been gone forever, as far as she knew; three months, in terms of his actual itinerary.

But he was home now—here, in the living room. His suitcases bulged with dirty laundry and curiosities, and were forgotten momentarily as his two daughters assailed him with questions and declarations:

"Cousin Bernie lost a tooth!" Johanna yelled.

Esther held her head up high for her announcement, "I know how to dry dishes now!" Then she added, "Did you see any sharks?"

Dad smiled and soaked in the waves of affection. Mom lingered in the corner, smoking a cigarette with a vacant look on her face. For the first time in three months, the questions weren't aimed at her.

"Mom, can I have ice cream?" Johanna asked.

The requests still were.

"I have an idea," Dad said, leaning in conspiratorially. "Why don't we have root beer floats?"

Esther and Johanna let out a unified cheer and marched towards the kitchen. There they found—almost like their parents had planned it—a tub of vanilla ice cream and a 2-liter of root beer. Mom pulled out plastic cups while Dad fished fished in the drawers for an ice cream scoop.

Cups fizzed and the two girls cheered. Their mom and dad exchanged significant looks while they shared in the laughter.

Esther held her cup close, the one shaped like a cowboy boot that she and her sister always fought over. The root beer bubbles glazed runny with ice cream, and she sat on the stairs, watching. Sleep called to her, and even as she fought it, the cup wilted in her chubby hands.

She woke partially on the way up the stairs, roused by the scratchy kiss placed on her forehead. Daddy was home. Vaguely aware of being stickier than usual, she cringed at the lukewarm washcloth applied to her chest and arms, and wondered what had become of her ice cream treat. She moved like a sleepy automaton, her arms in the air, receiving from somewhere a fresh nightgown.

Esther snuggled into her bed when she found herself there, holding tight to her blankie and humming absently. Sleep overwhelmed her.

And then the wretched dreams came.

Dust fell from the sky and consumed the air around her and beneath her. It was alive, crawling onto towers and trees and jettisoning itself onto unsuspecting people below, raining terror from the sky, and somehow bubbling up from the crevices of the earth at the same time until the entire human race was submerged…. The splash of water jarred her awake. Johanna was sitting on her bed, looking at once concerned and annoyed. "You woke me up."

Esther continued her usual summertime hours, exploring the bookshelves and corners inside, the crevices of the yard outside, ducking out of people's way when she saw them coming. She was embarrassed and frightened by her midnight dreams, but couldn't keep them from coming.

Every night she saw smokestacks coughing out thick layers of smoke; dust lined people's pockets and crawled out like bugs onto their hands when they waved at her in greeting.

Every night someone came to her: tenderly, like her father, or cross and impatient, like her mother or sister. The nightmares wouldn't stop coming. She ran to her parent's bed for safety but knew those days were numbered. Dad would leave again for work soon, and he was the one who let her under the covers. Her mom always sent her back to her room.

These experiences mortified her. Not because they haunted her during the day—she eyed people's pockets suspiciously, waiting for tiny puffs of air to erupt from anywhere they could be hidden—but because of the attention the episodes drew, whether it was good or bad. She hated the attention. She just wanted to be asleep, left alone.

And then one day it happened: something scary surfaced during daylight hours. Esther was sitting on the stairs silently watching her mother, who was cleaning the kitchen with the phone to her shoulder, talking with Aunt Jan. "Hot damn, that's a big 'un!" With a single, perfunctory motion, Esther's mother swept the spider into the vent with the broom in her hand.

Simple as that.

Esther blinked a few times. It was so simple! She knew just what to do.

She marched into her parents' bedroom where she'd seen a miniature, decorative broom, something Dad brought back from his latest trip. Asia, maybe? She seized it in her chubby little hands and took it to her room.

Every night from then on, she swept the perimeter of her bed, reaching into corners beneath the box spring. She'd rake it across her pillow and blankets for good measure, to be sure she'd rid her sleeping space of fodder for bad dreams.

She hummed absently as she undertook the ritual, days turning into weeks and then into months. Once, Esther noticed a long blue thread in the pile of debris. She plucked it from the detritus and studied it, recognizing it as the remainder of one of her dad's ties. The cat had destroyed it the week before, and even though her dad laughed, her mom nearly skinned the poor animal. Dad didn't have many nice ties.

Esther reached for her jewelry box, something her smoky grandmother had given her before she could remember. It still smelled like cigarettes. Inside, there were bottle caps and a few pennies, the corner of a candy bar wrapper that a cute boy from church had tossed aside, and some pencil erasers. She took the end of blue thread between her fingers, pieces of dust still attached to it, and watched it curl like a snake as she lowered it into its new home.

Eventually, her dad installed a hook where she could hang up the broom when she'd finished sweeping, and he affectionately referred to it as her "spider broom." It was what she used to chase away nightmares.

The tidier the space, the less room for monsters and uglies to hide.

Lithium Sandwich

There were probably ten of us in the room. We were free to go, except for the fact that the door was locked.

And so we waited.

The oranges they had us wear had a strange scent, like vomit mixed with tortilla. We filled them out differently, each one of us. It looked nice on the tanned-brown desert skin of a few of the girls, though it made the fat girl look like a Creamsicle. She seemed self-conscious about this, and covered what she could of herself with a wool blanket. It had the same vomit smell. She and another girl—practically an albino—sat on the metal bed, which was simply a block of metal built out from the wall.

Most of us tried to get as far away from the toilet as possible. None of us really wanted to look at it, though one girl pointed out bitterly, "There's not even toilet paper in here! How the fuck I'm s'posed to take a piss?"

"They lettin' us out soon." When this girl spoke I used it as an excuse to stare at the tattoo that trickled downward from her hairline, cut in front of her ear, then crept down her neck. She seemed comfortable, and was standing by the toilet using the crinkled aluminum foil mirror to finger-comb her stringy black hair. Strands of it drifted away from her hands and landed on an older woman sitting nearby, crumpled. I'd seen her when they brought her in. The blood on her face was cleaned away but the bruises were starting to show. She didn't move.

And we waited.

The biological imperatives arrived, and finally one of us, who just couldn't take it any longer, sat on the metal throne and stared into the middle distance while the stream rattled against the dented tin. I didn't want her to see me look at her, but I wanted to see the face of a woman who was pissing on a toilet surrounded by ten other women, ten strangers. She wobbled her hips over the rim, then leaned up onto the balls of her feet and bobbed her butt up and down like some nasty club dance.

Days like this I could see the benefit of being a man. Just piss anywhere. Shake it off. Resume normal duties.

Neck Tattoo got up and banged on the tiny window. "HEY! We need some mahfuggin toilet paper in here!"

Another girl threw her head back and shouted, "LET US OUT!" This one was painfully skinny, and I watched her knees knock against each other from the exertion of her scream. "I'm hungry, man." She snuffled and wiped her eyes. "About to get some nachos when I get out this bitch."

The albino sat with her legs crossed and her hands upturned on her knees. She lolled her head back with her eyes closed and looked like she was practicing drunken yoga. "Hungry," she breathed, then mouthed the word again and again. "Hungry. Hungry. Hungry."

A collective grimace. It had been at least twenty-four hours since any of us had eaten, and then it was just broth.

"Somebody tell her to shut up."

Knobby-knees sucked her teeth and glared. "She ain't even making noise. Leave her alone."

The pale girl kept rolling her head back, hitting the wall with a metallic *thud*. Her face sagged on its neck like an ill-fitting Halloween costume. Her mutters were barely-breathed whispers. "We hold these truths to be self-evident...no, no wait."

"Jesus, what's she saying?"

No one answered.

Neck Tattoo sighed loudly and stormed on the window again. "WHY AIN'T YOU LETTIN' US OUT?"

The blonde girl was making us uncomfortable. Before, we'd all just hugged our knees and stared at the floor in front of us. Don't ever make eye contact; that one we all learned quickly. But it had been quiet.

We were just waiting.

Now our stomachs pulled at the corners of our thoughts, tearing off sentences and leaving the thoughts incomplete. We were hungry.

"It is a truth...acknowledged..." She rocked her head back and forth, slowly. Her hands pawed clumsily at the air, grabbing at words that eluded her.

Then she shot straight up and smiled, triumphant. "A woman in want of a sandwich will make a sandwich!"

I chuckled in spite of myself, but it caught short in my throat like a sob. Neck Tattoo glared at me, and the fat girl looked worried. Knobby knees giggled unashamedly and called, "Ooooh, that bitch is crazy!"

"That girl needs some help." It was the girl who had pissed on the toilet. Somehow nothing she said mattered, because I'd seen her bob up and down over the toilet, and it was all I could see when she spoke. "I think she needs some meds."

"I was here all weekend, and she was here before me. They haven't given her any of her lithium since she's been in here." Fat girl said.

"She ain't on no lithium. Bitch is straight-up crazy." Knobby knees peeled off the fake nail on her ring finger and chucked it at the poor, muttering girl. Then she threw back her head and shouted, "LET US OUT!"

The albino began to mime.

She made fists in the air in front of her face, bent her elbows, and then moved her fists outward. No, they weren't fists—what was she doing?

At first we tried to ignore her, but it wasn't long before all of us were watching her every movement. It passed the time, and we were transfixed.

"She's opening doors!" I said.

"Shut up," Knobby Knees spat.

Pasty-face peered into the doors—or was it a window? She was looking hard for something. Her face lit up—aha! She'd found it—some sort of jug, the way her hand closed around it. She brought it close to her stomach and hunched her shoulders while twisting her hands in mid-air. Whatever she'd taken out of the imaginary door was hard to open.

There were more doors opening, and items gathered. She set them carefully on the metal around her, politely moving the fat girl's wool blanket from her workspace. Closing her eyes and humming, she waved one hand rhythmically over the other, as if she were buttering bread.

The preparations continued and became more elaborate. She squeezed, she poured, she sliced. She stirred something in a pot with one hand.

We watched, spellbound. Our stomachs rumbled and we glared at one another, daring anyone to say anything. Still, she did not open her eyes.

There were several invisible piles in front of her, and she took something from each one and laid it on the bread slices, now sitting invisibly on her lap. She'd piled everything on, added spices, and finally closed what could only be a sandwich. With both hands outstretched, barely containing the deli monstrosity, she inhaled with anticipation and offered a coy smile before unhinging her jaw for the first bite.

Her top teeth clicked on her bottom teeth, hard. Her eyes opened, and her bottom lip dropped.

It wasn't really a sandwich. There was nothing there.

Her eyes followed her hands, still in formation, down to her lap. Then everything crumbled. Her hands collapsed into her lap, and her chin fell to her chest.

Neck Tattoo stood up and moved around the small room like she owned it. She was laughing. "You tryin' to make a sandwich?" She stepped toward the albino and slapped at the curtain of hair in the girl's face. "Huh? You gonna share some of that Oscar Meyer shit up here?"

Knobby Knees joined the ridicule. "Her face look like mine done when I got my cherry popped!" She mimicked the phantom-sandwich and exaggerated the girl's shocked face. "Like, what the fuck was *that*?"

The albino didn't hear us. She rolled her shoulders and craned her neck at the walls and corners of the metal room, bewildered like a caged cat. The whites of her eyes rattled around. "I just want some food," she breathed.

The crumpled woman began to weep, though I don't know if she had been paying attention to any of us at all.

Neck Tattoo shook her head and pounded the knuckles of her clenched fist on the thigh of her orange-pants. "Man, but I am fucking hungry."

And then the howl again. "LET US OUT!"

The Women No One Sees

E sther was fourteen when she joined the ranks of the family cleaning business alongside her mother and older sister Johanna. Year after year, they'd pile into the minivan with the vacuum cleaner, dust mops and brooms, and various spray bottles organized haphazardly into buckets.

Squeegees and feather dusters poked akimbo from the mop pail like some sort of grotesque housecleaning mascot. Her mom and Johanna called it "The Mop Lady" and liked to laugh about it, "Did the Mop Lady take that gum?" But when Esther caught a glimpse of the Mop Lady in the corner of her eye, it startled her. Every time.

She had a cleaning caddy for herself that she kept neatly organized, armed with the supplies she'd need to dust and polish any surface. In her head, Esther called it the cleaning holster, and sometimes entertained herself having Windex quickdraw contests with her reflection.

Tonight, they were cleaning some building that had been repurposed at least three times, judging from the faded shapes on its front where different businesses had hung their logos.

No matter what the structure, it was their job to clean it, to make it look like no one had ever been in there.

***

Vivian wanted to shift her chair farther from the woman next to her, but they were those interlocked hotel conference chairs, so she was stuck. Normally the personal space thing didn't bother her so much, but she was here trying to take notes, trying to further her future, and this lady kept muttering nasty comments under her breath about the speaker, Allen Engle, and "this bullshit pyramid scheme."

It's not like that, Vivian wanted to hiss back at the woman. Allen was a great spokesperson with a powerful presence. She could admit that the products sometimes left a little to be desired, but mediocrity didn't bother her. It wasn't any better or worse than what she'd found at big-box stores.

"We're selling things people want and we're bringing it directly to them," Allen had told her. "The truth is, it's not all magnificent. But we are consumers of crap, let's just face it. We need these products to fill the part of our soul we're trying to stuff Cheetos into, you know?"

Oh, she knew. He didn't have to tell her twice. No one needed these cosmetics, these facial masks, these hair crimper-slash-curling-irons or three-brushes-in-one. But they were marketed with "a nurturing care and a personal touch that no store could ever hope to duplicate." Even if it was a line from the sales guide, it was one she believed in.

Like Allen always said, Vehemence was a family, and it was a family dedicated to making women feel good about themselves. Everything else in the world made them feel like they fell short. Here was something that could really empower them.

Vivian wasn't entirely convinced she needed a straightening iron to empower herself, but she didn't know what else would, aside from maybe being the one who was selling them.

And so she sold. She sold enough in the first year to attract the attention of some of the higher-ups, and she'd been invited to two regional conferences now. This time they'd even paid for her room and she was going to share a meal with a few of the speakers, including Allen. She'd bought a mock turtleneck sweater from the consignment shop just for the occasion.

Vivian knew better than to lie to herself about why she was so excited. Allen was a charismatic speaker, and his looks added to his allure. The first thing she'd noticed about him were his dark, flirtatious eyebrows set in contrast to his short sandy hair. He must have known they were his best feature, because he used them to emphasize and exaggerate his expressions.

God, I'm such a cliché, she thought, shaking her head. Single mom at a product-sales conference, getting her vitals twisted up over some collared shirt and tie.

And khakis.

***

They were a machine, the three of them. When Mrs. Eisenmann had called them about the new property, to warn them it was high maintenance and that they should set aside at least two hours to clean it, their smug smiles were warranted.

"Don't you worry, Mrs. E." Esther's mom flicked her cigarette ashes into the bowl by the phone. "You know me and my girls will have the whole place sparkling in under an hour."

Some places were amazed the three women could complete the job so quickly. The manager at the law office went so far as calling the security company to verify their log in and log out times.

They had a rhythm, that was all—even in the way they entered the building. Each plotted the quickest course to their destination and they mobilized, turning on lights and turning off alarm systems in a methodical cadence, then getting to work.

Mom handled the bathrooms, Johanna went straight for the dust mop, and Esther took care of the trash. When the last of the garbage had been emptied, she'd whip out some polish and a microfiber rag from her bucket and march into the offices. No photo frame untouched; keyboards and mouse pads wiped—then lifted, to reach the surface beneath them.

They weaved around one another, offering encouragements when there was something particularly gross or unheard of, and making comments like, "Uh oh, the popcorn bandit is back!" They knew the secretary was off her diet again when the floor under her desk was littered with the pethy, microwaved snack.

***

Allen stood up halfway and waved to her from his table in the corner of the hotel restaurant. His teeth practically sparkled in the dim lighting.

"Vivian, hello!" He touched her elbow and placed a friendly kiss on her cheek. The gesture seemed exotic to her. It was something people did in Europe or in the movies. She'd been expecting a handshake and now was more flustered than she wanted to admit.

"You'll have to forgive Shawn. She got called back to Cleveland this morning. She really wanted to sit down and talk with you, too—" he frowned and pointed at the look of doubt on Vivian's face. She didn't believe him, but she certainly liked the way it sounded. "No, no, it's true. And they're talking about you back at HQ. The rising star!"

He raised his eyebrows and gave the waiter a nod from across the room. "I hope you don't mind white."

"White?" Since the peck on the cheek, Vivian had only managed to communicate through an awkward series of grimaces and bashful smiles. *Use your words, Viv.* "Oh, wine? Yes—yes, that sounds lovely. Thank you."

Allen sipped from his water glass, never taking his eyes from her. Certain he was waiting for her to say something else, Vivian offered a few head nods and inhalations that never quite formed into words. The whole thing—the kiss, the lighting, the wine—it didn't feel like the "business success dinner" the Vehemence secretary had described on the phone.

"Vivian?"

"Yes?"

Allen gave her an appraising look. The homely brunette was very nearly receding into her turtleneck sweater, head down and shoulders hunched. He completely understood why Leonard thought she'd be the perfect person for the job. The perfect mixture of self-doubt and self-loathing, plus a dash of hot mess.

"Please don't be nervous." He smiled softly to himself, remembering that he was the perfect person for his job, too. The finesse.

Thinking his expression was meant as a comfort, she took it. It worked, too. She felt heartened. "I swear, Allen, I'm not usually this awkward. I just, well … "

The waiter filled their wine glasses and Vivian stared at the microscopic beads of water forming a cool cloud on the outside of the glass. She watched Allen's eyebrows waggle with their own vocabulary as he first took a curious sip, then an appreciative one.

Once he had set his glass down, she counted slowly in her head, all the way to ten, before taking her own first sip. The crisp liquid's bite on her tongue was worth the wait. She set the glass down and began counting again in her head, being sure to nod at intervals and "mmhmm" as Allen began his monologue. Three sips in, she felt the warmth of the alcohol spreading its hot fingers around her blood vessels. It climbed them like ropes, hand over hand, into each of her extremities.

"Vivian? Is everything okay?"

She took another swallow of wine before realizing he was waiting for a response to something he'd said. "Yes, I'm sorry. There's—you're saying there's a new product line?"

"Well, a new demographic. And you're the perfect candidate for launching its inaugural run right here in town. What do you think? Want to hear more?"

Vivian nodded one more time, this time with a wide, warm smile covering her face.

"That's what I hoped for, Viv." Allen motioned to the waiter again. "Let's order some dinner. You like crab cakes?"

***

It had been about four weeks—four separate cleanings—of the new place when Mrs. Eisenmann stopped by their house to tell them the facility manager was nervous about the size of their cleaning entourage.

"I told him you all were our best team," Mrs. Eisenmann took the cup of tea Maggie offered. "But I guess he's the nervous type. Start-up company and all."

Johanna rolled her eyes. "Old Mr. Uglykids just has pent up energy."

The older woman nearly slid off the couch, eyeballing Esther's giggling sister. "*What* did you call him?"

"Ha! You didn't know? We got pet names for all of them." Johanna counted off on her fingers. "There's Popcorn Lady, Casanova, Hoarder…now we have Mr. Uglykids."

Esther smiled and said quietly, "He's a great addition to the collection."

Johanna's giggle morphed into an ugly squawk. "Have you met the dude who's in charge? Oh my god, the pictures on his desk," she snorted again. "They are *startlingly* ugly children. No wonder he's got a beef. I'd be mad too, if my kids looked like that."

Esther snorted in spite of herself, and the sisters laughed even harder when they made eye contact with one another.

"*Girls!*" Their mother's smoky baritone startled them, and they both sat up straight. Once their mother was satisfied they'd calmed down, she turned her attention back to her employer. "I don't understand. He doesn't want all three of us there?"

It was Mrs. Eisenmann's turn to roll her eyes. "It's a strange facility and he seems a strange man, but he pays the top rate. Can just one of you clean it?" She set her tea down on the table, throwing a sidelong glance at the teenagers. "And ladies, no more nicknames, okay?"

The second their mother stepped towards the front door with Mrs. Eisenmann, Johanna and Esther melted off the couch and ran from the room in hysterics.

***

The waiter filled their wine glasses again when he brought out their dinners. Allen went with the crab cakes and onion rings; Vivian supposed she might look sensible if she ordered a salad, so she went with the Cobb. She tried to eat it one tiny piece at a time like the actresses in romantic comedies. But wouldn't they do the thing where they order a giant greasy burger and not gain a pound, and go into hysterics after belching at the table? What kind of woman did Allen prefer?

"I'm telling you, you have got to try one of these." Allen bit down on one of the onion rings and the onion slid right out of the crusty casing, giving him a greasy slap on the chin. He wiped it with a grunt.

Vivian scraped at some lettuce. "Oh, I've got plenty here, thanks. But tell me more about these new products—"

"*Mmm,*" Allen interrupted her, though his mouth was full of food. He put his finger up to indicate she should wait while he swallowed, which he did with a painful grimace. "Sorry, hot bite. There is no new product. We're just switching up our audience."

"Oh?" She popped a cherry tomato in her mouth and hoped it looked cute.

"That's right. We here at Vehemence, we're a family, you know? We want—" he stopped mid-sentence and hung his head. "Gosh, just listen to me. I don't need to go into sales mode with you. You're already a part of the family, you know that." He flashed a smile and reached across the table to pat her hand.

Vivian was halfway through glass number two. His touch was warm and she leaned forward as an invitation for more of that sort of thing. "You don't need to sell me anything, Allen. Just tell me what to do."

"What we want to do is cater specifically to lower income brackets. The market's locked on your standard suburban housewife. But what about the women who get overlooked, the ones no one seems to see?"

This time he grabbed her hand with both of his and looked into her face. "I see you, Vivian. I know it's a struggle, raising a child by yourself—"

Vivian pulled away reflexively at this, using the hand he'd touched to take another gulp of wine. Marky was upstairs in the room right now, watching *Seinfeld* reruns. She couldn't afford a sitter, and besides, neither one of them wanted to pass up the indoor pool and free HBO.

"So, you're marketing to single moms?"

"It's more than that, Vivian. Bigger. *The women no one seems to see.*" He paused for effect and Vivian nodded, trying to understand. "Sure, it's the single moms. But it's the ones in the programs, too, your alkies, junkies. Battered women in shelters."

Vivian was mid-sip when he mentioned "alkies" and looked up at him from her glass, but Allen was lost in his pitch. "These women deserve access to our products—we want to take our business to them. It's sort of a 'fake it till you make it.' If they can feel better about themselves on the outside, maybe things will improve for them on the inside."

The waiter approached to clear their plates and Allen motioned for two more glasses of wine, though he didn't take his eyes off of Vivian while she processed the information. She had a face like she smelled something funny, but couldn't quite place it. He wondered how many aces he'd have to pull out before she agreed. She would agree soon enough. And not even with an ace—maybe not even a face card.

"It's not like they don't have access to our products, I don't think. It's just…it's not a priority. These women got a different view on what comes first."

"Of course, of course," Allen nodded gravely. "But don't you think they deserve to have the choice? It's not on their radar because it's too far away. We want to put the product in their proximity."

Vivian gestured with her wine glass as she spoke. "Okay. But how exactly do you plan to target them? You're saying they're not already in the sales funnel?" She hoped that was the right terminology.

"That's where you come in. We want you to do a little…outreach."

Vivian took a few swallows of wine, then set the glass down and traced her fingers on the stem. "I don't know, Allen. Am I even qualified? And I'm not sure I have the flexibility…" she trailed off and took another drink.

His partner Leonard had been right about the wine, Allen thought, watching her wave down the waiter. The woman really could put it away. "It's delicate, but from what you've told me about your background, you might have some…perspective." Vivian looked down at her hands. It was time to take a step closer. "Are you worried about time away from … it's Mark, isn't it?" He watched as her eyes snapped up. *Bingo.*

"How did you—? I never told you his name."

"Shawn told me." He gave a little wave of his hand. "Like I said, we've been talking about you. He's upstairs now, right? In the room?"

Vivian froze. "Wait, what? I mean, I checked into it, and by law—"

Allen leaned forward and took her hands, both of them this time. "Hey, hey. Vivian, it's okay. Look at me." He waited until her eyes landed on his face, then continued. "We want you to have this opportunity because you and Mark deserve it. It's going to change things for both of you. Say, change of title, give you a spot on the payroll?"

She sat back in her chair, her thoughts a bit soupy after the third glass of wine. Maybe it was the fourth. "So, I get a permanent position. You—the company—gets to move in a new direction with a new demographic."

Allen gave a curt nod, but said nothing. He stared at her intently, his eyebrows raised in question.

"What if it doesn't work? What if I fail?"

"Honestly, Viv? I don't see how you could. Let's shake on it."

Vivian took a sip from her freshly filled wine glass and pointed at him, glass still in hand. "And here I thought you was going to kiss me again."

***

When the dusting was finished, Esther would typically join her sister with a mop, the two of them swaying in a silent, focused rhythm as the soggy tendrils of Mop Lady hair rolled languidly across the surface of the floor. It made Esther think of the woman with the alabaster jar, using her hair to wash Jesus' feet. The white noise of the vacuum would hold them all in their own thoughts, the two daughters mop-dancing, their mother pushing the sweeper back and forth with a pendulous flourish.

There was none of that, now that Esther was cleaning the facility by herself. She didn't mind in the least; in fact, she welcomed the solitude. It let her snoop a little. Usually, if she even looked at a picture too long, her mom would bark from across the room, or land a heavy palm across the back of Esther's head.

But now, she did more than look at pictures. She took them from their frames to see what had been scrawled on the back; she rooted gently through unlocked drawers and peeked in the fridge. All of these people, leading their lives completely unaware of her.

At the same time, though, they traveled in separate dimensions than she did. They were just as invisible to her. The thing she daydreamed about more than anything else was what she would do if she ever ran into one of the faces from the photos, in person.

Out front, the minivan honked. She'd taken too long. Snapping to attention, she conducted a guilty walk-through, inspecting her work and eyeing carpeted corners for any fuzzy speck that would malign their cleaning reputation.

And there was one, right there along the back wall leading to their janitor's closet. Esther bent to pick it up but saw it was just a miniscule blotch of sinkwater-gray paint. She scratched at it but it was good and stuck. It must have splashed there when they painted the wall. From the looks of it, it had been a while.

Her mom would be impatient, so she'd have to leave it for the next time. She ran out to the car and as they drove away, she still wondered about the people who worked there during the day. She wondered if they thought about her.

That's when she noticed the section at the back of the building without any windows. Esther mentally traced her route through the building. Each of the three offices on that side had a window, and then, if she were walking down the hall, it would turn and lead to their janitor closet. When she'd been standing in that hallway by the newly painted wall, she thought that was the end of the building. Here, from the outside, she saw that it extended beyond that. There was easily enough space for another room, maybe two.

***

It was harder than Vivian thought it would be. Over the next several weeks she scoured the area for women's shelters, psychiatric wards, places where she might find the women Allen wanted her to find.

At the local behavioral health center, she didn't even make it past registration; if she had moved a little more slowly she was fairly certain the nurse would have kicked her on the way out. The ladies at the women's shelter office listened to Vivian's spiel, and handled a few of the products.

One of the outreach coordinators, Linnea, was a stick-thin little thing with a pierced nose and jet-black hair so straight it looked like daggers exiting the Celtic hair barrette. She picked up the three-in-one hair styler. "This looks like a fancy hair doohickey. It doesn't just fall apart after a few tries though, does it?"

"Oh, absolutely not. I've had mine for two years now, and it's what I used to flip my hair out before coming here." Vivian patted her hair. "You really need to see how quickly it heats up, too. Do you mind if I plug it in?"

"Sandy?" The young woman threw a questioning look at the mousy, brittle-haired woman leaning against the doorframe, and Vivian guessed that Sandy was in charge.

"We're slow enough. You want to play dress-up, you go ahead." Sandy's pleated jeans didn't fit her quite right, making it the faded green t-shirt's job to cover the fleshwaves spilling out over the waistband.

Linnea and Vivian crowded the electrical outlet like co-conspirators, making their plans for Linnea's hair.

"So plate the hair this way if you want to straighten it, turn it on the side for a flip-out..." Vivian reached back into the box. "And look, it's really almost four-in-one, since you can attach this crimper."

"I hear crimping is coming back in," Linnea said, laughing. She let out a giggle when she released the handle and found three inches of her hair perfectly ridged like a potato chip.

Sandy rolled her eyes as she watched them, but there was a smile on her face. "Yeah, our ladies might get a kick out of this. A self-esteem boost, confidence at job interviews. Your company—what's it called again, Adamant?—is doing a great thing, making these donations."

"It's Vehement," Vivian frowned. "I'm sorry, maybe there's been a misunderstanding. We're rolling out a reduced-price feature for women in difficult situations, but we're not exactly *donating....*"

The tenor of the room changed, then. Linnea set the crimper down and stole a look at Sandy, who had unfolded her arms and was now leaning forward on the desk where Vivian sat.

"Look, I appreciate what you think you're trying to do, but you're missing the mark."

Linnea nodded in agreement. "We run on *donations*, and hell, we're barely running. Companies giving us their discontinued or expired makeup. Rich ladies give us their old suits. Half our ladies are lucky if they have a winter coat. You want them to pay ten dollars for a—" she scoffed, midsentence, "a *hair crimper?*"

Vivian started to gather her things, the shame radiating from her like heat waves. They were right. They were absolutely right and that's what she had tried to tell Allen, but he wouldn't listen.

She managed a stifled, "thank you for your time, ladies" before leaving the room, her head buried in her bag like she was searching for her keys. She was trying to hide the tears she knew were coming.

Not so many years before, she'd been in a facility just like this one. St. Margaret's. That was when the state had taken Marky from her, after Brian had died. The ladies at Maggie's had given her a place to sleep and volunteers ran workshops on job application skills, parenting. They'd given her a way to stand on her own two feet again.

Here she was, thinking she'd come back to a women's shelter as some sort of success story, or like, her way of giving back. And the whole thing had fallen flat. She'd screwed the whole thing up. Of course they were right. This was a horrible place to give a pitch. It was completely inappropriate.

But what was she going to do? Vivian had visited local Al Anon and NA chapters, the hospitals, hell, even a few bookstores. None of them wanted anything to do with her "skeezy pyramid scheme," as the bookstore owner had called it.

It was going to be a tough phone call to Allen and Leonard the next morning, that much she was sure of.

***

Dusting was Esther's favorite. No giant pail of soapy water to slosh down the hall; no extension cord to unravel. Not even an "on" button. Just a light rag, dampened with Windex—sometimes orange cleaner.

It smelled slightly sweet and slightly sharp, and she secretly loved when she smelled it on her clothes at the end of the night, mixed in with the little bit of sweat she'd worked up. Sometimes she'd set it to "spray" and give one pump into the air before walking through it, like it was Bulgari perfume. She was pretty sure Bulgari was expensive, because it came in a very fancy bottle and laid inside an even fancier box.

Esther knew this because the receptionist kept some in her top drawer. After cleaning the place by herself the first time, Esther took a piece of candy from the bowl on the desk and sat in the spinny chair. The box's lid shimmered from inside the partially-open drawer. It wouldn't close completely on account of all of the other junk the lady kept in there.

In subsequent weeks, Esther would carefully lift the lid and remove the bottle from its perfectly molded indentation. It was heavy, and crescendoed into a swirled mob of clear crystal at the top.

She'd close her eyes and breathe deeply at the opening, inhaling her way to some gondola in a foreign country where people rode bikes everywhere and the car horns sounded different, and the pigeons were white instead of gray. Then she'd wrap her finger in an unsoiled portion of her rag and Windex her fingerprints from the bottle before placing it sweetly back into its case, making sure the nozzle pointed the same direction as she'd found it.

Her heart always ached when she walked away. She was a ghost, as a cleaner, an unthanked face who dealt with people's personal belongings on a daily basis. But this particular item she coveted from a place deep within her she had not known existed; a place that was as foreign to her as the white pigeons in her perfume-induced daydream.

***

"We're not philanthropists, sweetheart."

Leonard's voice had a way of making Vivian understand how a dog felt when someone pet it backwards, against the grain. It sent a shudder to her kneecaps and back. She'd never met him in person, but Allen brought him in on some of their calls. Something in his voice seethed contempt. She could never say the right thing, as far as he was concerned.

"No, I don't think we should be giving product away, neither. But this model isn't really working, or our approach—"

"This is *your* approach, isn't it? We've given you a lot of freedom and leeway—and a hell of a paycheck—but we're not seeing any results."

There was an audible sigh and then some muffled sounds on the other end, like someone had covered the phone's speaker. Allen's voice came over next. Gentler. More patient. Vivian hugged her phone closer to her ear to drink it in. She hadn't been given a lot of kindness over the past few weeks.

"I told you I wanted to reach a new group, the women no one sees. You can reach them. We need you to reach them. So what can you do differently, Viv?"

This stopped her. She'd tried to straighten it all out in her head, but the truth was, she wasn't so business smart. And she'd needed a few drinks to steel herself for this conversation, so she wasn't at her sharpest. "Well, I—I…I was thinking…" She was thinking that, for the life of her, she still didn't understand why they'd tasked her with something so monumental.

Leonard snorted. "You're done thinking. It's not your forte. Here's the plan: You need to get us a test group. Asses in seats. Ten of them."

Allen cut in again to explain. "We want to have a product demo, and we want your ladies to be our guinea pigs—don't use that phrase with *them*, of course. But listen, when I said I didn't think you'd fail, I meant it." he paused, then his voice gained a sharper edge. "There's no room for it."

Vivian was sitting on the edge of the tub, hunched over. Her insides squirmed. A test group? What product demo? This wasn't what she'd been asked to do.

She passed Marky on her way to the kitchen. He was sprawled on the couch in his dad's old Browns jersey, laughing and talking into his headset to a few of his friends, as she grabbed the bottle from the top of the fridge. He was too busy scrolling through his phone to even notice the aliens from his video game splattered on the screen.

She took a hot swig without bothering to find a glass. "I don't want to let you down, Allen. Leonard. You want new clients and I'll—"

Leonard interrupted her. "Forget clients. I'll speak slowly so you understand. We need disadvantaged females. Your job is to get us a demo group."

Vivian felt the anger rising in her. Her mentors at St. Margaret's had told her not to let people treat her like she was stupid. She deserved better.

"I can do my job better if you wouldn't change the objective midstream!"

This time Allen's voice was as sharp as Leonard's. "The objective has changed, Viv, since we're done with your screwing around. Just get asses in seats, ten of them, in two weeks. This has to happen because my ass is riding on it, which means your ass is riding on it."

Vivian sank against the wall, staring at the ceiling with big bubble tears in her eyes. She couldn't deliver. It was that simple. She sniffled and gave a breathy, "Okay, Allen. I'll try."

"Try?" Leonard's sneer was palpable in his tone. "It's been pretty nice with this hefty new paycheck, hasn't it? Fattened up that chunky boy of yours some more. What is he, twelve?"

Her stomach went cold, and Vivian felt the chilly tingle rise up her spine to her neck where the hairs rose up like antenna, sniffing the air.

That was the thing that had been digging in her mind like a splinter ever since having dinner with Allen at the hotel. She'd thought about it a few times since then, thought about how she drank too much and flirted like a buffoon. Thought about whether or not she'd ever talked to Shawn, or anyone, about Marky.

She was pretty sure she hadn't. And she sure as hell hadn't told anyone that he was a chunky twelve-year-old.

Something was wrong.

Who were these men? "This conversation is making me uncomfortable. What are you trying to say?"

"What we're trying to say is that we don't like to be disappointed," Leonard said.

"What the hell, guys? I thought this was a family, isn't that what you're always spouting?"

Allen let out a slow laugh. "And tell 'Marky' that the Browns suck."

The line was dead.

This wasn't good.

Vivian took off her hoodie and threw it to the floor, then jammed the faucet on cold, full blast. Bending over the countertop, she dipped her head into the sink and felt the water gush onto her scalp. It ran down her face, making icy rivulets of foundation and mascara on her cheeks.

There isn't time to waste, she told herself.

"Marky?" she called, walking into the living room. "I'm going to need your help."

The two of them crouched in front of the laptop for the next few hours. Vivian had a hard enough time making friends in real life, she'd never fussed with social media. She needed help to set up a group and send invitations, but only after Marky had created a profile for her.

She tilted her head at the screen. "So, I just put my stupid mug up there and ask people to like it?"

"Well, you don't want to *ask* for likes. That's what creepy people do and it always sounds desperate." Mark looked at his mother. "Here, take your hair down. Let me take your picture."

Vivian rubbed her face with her sleeve to wipe away any melted makeup. "Oh god. In this? And I just soaked my head in the sink."

"Jesus, mom. Why'd you do that?" He smirked, then saw her face. She was tired, and stressed out. This new job seemed to be wearing on her, even if it had gotten them some pretty sweet electronics. "Mom, you're really pretty. You have a trustworthy face. People will see it, and see what you're doing…they'll be happy to join up."

He reached over and scrunched her hair a little. "There. Now, just smile a little bit, not some big stupid grin. No—that's a grimace. You look like you're about to take a dump!"

Vivian laughed in spite of herself, the easy, open-mouth laugh she could only share with her son. He snapped the photo right away, capturing the moment perfectly on the screen. She looked like she was having fun, enjoying where she was in life. And, in the split second that laugh had taken place, she probably was.

That whole weekend, she gathered and posted promotional material—inspirational quotes, product information. It was flimsy, but enough to limp on. When it came to sending invitations, she scoured local pages that offered the same type of support and wellness information as the brick-and-mortar facilities she'd visited in the last few weeks—women's shelters, pages devoted to drug abuse recovery, victim support, that sort of thing.

The results were immediate. Vivian crunched caramel popcorn and watched the screen as notifications lit up every few minutes or so. Monday afternoon, she reached next to her on the couch for the phone and dialed Allen.

"Tell me you've got something, Viv."

"I think I did it, Allen. There's three dozen people signed onto my Facebook group, and I'm waiting to hear back from double that."

"Wow, darlin', sounds like you really turned that around. Soak it up while you can, this sweet scent of success." He no longer had any emotion in his voice, and it chilled Vivian. "Oh, I'll let you go. Looks like Marky is home."

Vivian whipped her head around and saw the clock. It was just after three o'clock and there—she drew the shades back on the second story apartment window—the school bus had stopped on the street out front.

"Listen, sorry we had to put the pressure on you the other night. I guess even families fight sometimes, right?" Allen gave a dry chuckle. "Maybe I can work in some sort of bonus for you. You've earned it."

"What the hell is this, Allen? What do you want with Marky?" She had sunk to her knees on the floor, covering her face with her free hand. "Please, just leave us alone."

"I don't want anything with Marky. But it's just a damn good way to make sure this gets done, don't you think? Do the job, Viv. See you next week."

Vivian threw the phone before she heard anything else, then ran to her bedroom to hide her frantic tears. Marky couldn't know anything was wrong.

***

Standing in the bathroom-turned-custodial-closet, Esther waited for the stained yellow bucket to fill with sudsy mop water. It was easy enough to stay busy, pressing her finger through the cloth into the corrugation of each cleaning product bottle. They'd been there for years, she guessed; some of them had crusted themselves to the rickety shelves.

Curious, Esther opened a tricenarian Pine-Sol to see if it would smell the same as a fresh bottle, but she fumbled the cap. It clacked along the chrome bars of the shelving unit before careening into the hollow death rattle only a plastic cap can make as it comes to a standstill.

She bent to retrieve it behind the forgotten, grody toilet and stopped. Some type of warranty was stuck to the tank, but the tape had yellowed, and where the paper leaned away from its adhesive prison, someone had written on it in tiny, faint print.

***

It was a dismal, nondescript building, with faded spots on its exterior. Vivian double-checked the address on the index card before walking in. It was almost over.

Ten women had confirmed their arrival at the facility for a demo of Vehemence's new product line. She'd gotten "asses in seats." That conversation still rang in her head daily. Something was wrong, she knew it. They'd changed the plan on her, for one thing. And the other thing—well, she'd sent Marky to stay with her brother in Michigan.

This wasn't what she'd signed up to do. But she'd done it, and in the end that was what mattered. It was a good day.

"Vivian, right?" The woman at the front desk eyed a clipboard. "They want to see you before you go in. Right this way please, ma'am."

Vivian wasn't used to a well-dressed woman calling her "ma'am." It felt pretty good. The receptionist took her to an office where Allen and another man—Leonard, Vivian guessed—were seated behind a table.

"Morning, Viv," Allen said, offering a smile. Leonard looked bored.

"I guess this is it, right? The ladies should be here soon." Vivian began to stammer when neither man acknowledged her. "Will you need me in the demo room, or should I just be greeting..." She trailed off when Allen got up to close the door. "Is something wrong?"

"I guess it gets tricky now," Leonard said. It was definitely Leonard. That thin, nasally voice made her hairs stand on end. He walked to her side of the table. "We want you to be a part of the demo, sure."

Allen's eyes danced between Leonard and Vivian. "Your face is pretty recognizable. The other women know your face from the group profile."

Vivian frowned. "Well, sure. But I've got a trustworthy face, right?"

The two men were quiet for a moment before Allen said, "We're afraid it could skew results."

None of it made any sense to Vivian, what they said next. She hardly understood social media, let alone what the hell would go on during the demo, but they were telling her the women might be angry with her when they saw her, if they recognized her.

"Maybe I just don't participate?"

"Oh no," Leonard chuckled dangerously. "That simply isn't an option."

The details, the explanations, all of them fuzzed out after the first punch to the face. It knocked her from her chair and left droplets of blood on the floor. *What the HELL?* Vivian had blubbered, and thrown out some other choice words. The best ones she knew.

Allen bent over and guided her back to her seat, speaking softly. "It will hurt, Viv. But this will work out better for you. Trust me." He took one of her hands in his and kissed it softly, shushing her tears, then slapped her sharply with his other hand. Her cry came out like a bark, and she sobbed incoherently after that.

"Both eyes and a cheek, that oughta do it." Leonard's snakeskin voice interrupted Vivian's tears. "Now, how about that hair?"

She thought of Marky while they lopped her hair off in great chunks using some scissors the receptionist delivered. He used to play with her chocolate tresses back when she could still call them that, before age and stress and drink turned them into the brittle wands she had now. He would lay on her lap in just his diaper and she'd tickle his belly with the full, weighty strands of her hair.

The receptionist—a surly woman now, no more of this "ma'am" stuff—led her down a hallway into a nondescript office. A man in a medical coat ran a quick examination, shrugging as he jotted down some numbers, then jabbed a syringe of something into her shoulder.

Rough hands shoved her into a metallic, sterile-looking room. Vivian couldn't make much out through her swollen eyes, but heard the furtive whispers of a few female voices before the door shut and everything went dark.

***

Some date. I don't know.

Maybe no one will ever read this but I have to say I'm sorry.

These women are here because of me, and I don't know what's going to happen to us.

It was just a job. But now they have us in these cells. I can't talk to any of them, can't even look at them. What if they know I'm the one who brought them here?

God forgive me, I know the one girl needs some medicine. She wasn't stable and made for an easy sell. The others I just lied to. I told them if they bought this stuff from me, I could get them selling it too. Money for rent and food. Birthday parties. I used his lines on them and it worked.

It's like prison but worse. Orange suits. Broth. One by one they take a girl and when she comes back she's...different. There testing something on us, and keep saying there getting us ready for the demo.

I reached out to poor people and addicts and victims. He said the women no one sees but he meant the ones no one would miss.

If you read this remember us. We were here. God forgive me.

***

It was several months later, and Esther stole into the building from the rooftop. After she'd read the mysterious letter and learned of the false wall, she'd taken time each week to find a way in. She had to get to it, that's all she knew.

There was no way she'd just bust in through the wall—too much to clean up. And she didn't want to tell anyone. What if it was nothing? Besides, Esther loved a secret. She wondered if she'd found someone else invisible, like her.

Once she knew to look, it wasn't hard to get to. There was an extra room in back. She couldn't get in from the inside wall or the outside wall, so she tried it from above, dropping in from a vent. Like Macguyver, Johanna would have said.

She hadn't been surprised to find the bodies. A few sprawled across metal cots, a few on the floor; the women's faces were dusty, skeletal sloths stretched into various grimaces. There were eleven of them.

It took her a few weeks to come up with a plan. First, she made sure she didn't clean there anymore. And not her mom or Johanna. Then, she knew she needed to send them off properly, the women.

Esther kneeled beside one of them and studied the ancient-looking groan as she felt the bottle of Bulgari perfume in her pocket. She'd avoided tripping the alarm when she stole it outright, but knew the finger would point to the cleaning crew. They'd lost the job.

For someone without access to money or fine things, it was worth it. The bottle's lure was too strong, and it seemed to Esther the only way to honor the contents—the women—of this tragic chamber.

She opened the perfume, the strong scent of a foreign world bathing the silent place. Like the woman with the alabaster jar, she poured its contents, a trickle at a time, at the feet of each body. It was all that she had to offer.

And yet, it was clear to her, it wasn't enough. Their faces cried out to her, remember us. Take us with you. Esther took her fingernail and scraped at the dusty skull in front of her, holding the empty perfume bottle beneath it. She did this to each body, each face, until the bottle was brimming with it, though she couldn't tell if it was ashes or dust. *Same thing*, she thought.

Then she pocketed the vial and made her way out of the silent, reluctant tomb.

Vermin

I t was slow for a peak-season Thursday. Sophie clicked and typed behind the front desk counter to check in Mr. Owsinski, the weekly regular, into his favorite room, 116. The front desk girl had a dazzling smile that always disappeared immediately once the guests turned away.

Esther loitered in a corner of the cavernous lobby, dust mop in hand, while a scattering of guests chatted over beers on the stain-resistant, patterned couches. Large glass windows spanned one whole wall of the room and welcomed the sun in the daytime. Aside from that, the only view they offered was the end-to-end traffic of the city's most dangerous intersection. Their parking lot often played host to emergency vehicles.

Mrs. Rose was small, so Sophie could only see the top of her head over the front desk counter, and half of it was buried in the older woman's oversized bag as she searched through its contents for her credit card. It was something of a Mary Poppins purse, and Mrs. Rose drove home the hyperbole by commenting out loud to herself on each item she came across: "I need to put that ticket stub in my scrapbook. That was a good movie…I'm glad I saw it with Benjamin. He gets that sort of thing."

Some of the items ended up on the turquoise formica, placed carefully by a dry hand with ridged fingernails. A crinkled tissue. A tube of chapstick lined with lint where the label was peeled back, exposing the adhesive. Hotel pens with the old company logo. The place hadn't been a Sheraton in years.

"I need to get a purse to have inside my purse so I can organize all of those things together."

"Yeah," Sophie chuckled politely, eyeing the clock on her computer monitor. A rerun of her favorite show would be on soon. "Sometimes I think I should just carry around a tacklebox."

For a moment the rummaging paused. The woman peered upwards at Sophie, eyebrow first, with a curious expression. It seemed she considered a response, but thought better of it, or didn't think about it long enough, because she returned her focus to rustling inside of the bag.

After a few moments, she looked up with that same eyebrow and was reminded of the task at hand. "Yes, the hotel. I use the Mastercard here, don't I?"

Sophie scrolled through the record of Mrs. Rose's visits, eyeing the payment column. "Looks like you've used the Mastercard for the last three visits, but before that, you used the Discover card."

Another pause, Mrs. Rose's hand clutching some unnamed item inside of the great bag. The dark brows twitched and the woman removed the hand to brush a phantom hair from her eyes. "I keep forgetting that I keep it short now," she muttered.

For the sake of time, Sophie checked Mrs. Rose in, despite her inability to find the card. The woman had stayed enough times that her credit was in good standing. Besides, experience told Sophie that Mrs. Rose would find her card the moment she set her bag down, or went back out to her car. She was known for banging on the metal pull-down window, which was reserved for afterhour check-ins, to present a credit card or return a plastic keycard from a previous stay.

"With all the money I've spent here in the last year, I could have put a deposit down on a new apartment," Mrs. Rose had grumbled one morning while Sophie set up the breakfast counter. There were only a few guests there at that hour, staring bleary-eyed into their coffee cups. "I wish that jerk of a landlord would take care of those raccoons."

She stayed at the hotel because her apartment complex had a raccoon problem, and she had a sleeping problem. On the nights when the combination became unbearable, she checked in. She was a good guest, as guests went. Aside from the occasional 4 am delivery of a credit card, no one ever saw her once she'd gone to her room.

Mrs. Rose stopped rummaging and looked at Sophie with renewed focus. "I'd like to make a reservation, too. Can you help me with that?"

This was new. She'd never prearranged for a room before, in fact there had been more than one evening during the busy summer when they'd had to turn her away because the rooms were booked—no, they couldn't rent the utility room for her, they were sorry to say.

"My son is coming to visit. He doesn't like my apartment because he hates my landlord and the raccoons more than I do." She fumbled idly through the Mary Poppins bag, though it seemed more out of habit than any specific intention.

"It will be a pleasure to meet him, Mrs. Rose. I'll make sure that he gets the VIP treatment!" Sophie's voice dripped with buttered curiosity. There would be a long note in the log-book at the end of the shift, for sure. Maybe even be a few bubble letters.

Mrs. Rose looked up at Sophie for a moment and seemed about to say something, but smiled widely and said, "There's a new episode of *SVU* coming on. I'll be in my room if you need me."

"Thanks, Mrs. Rose. Have a good evening."

***

Esther had run a set of towels to a guest and returned to the lobby where she planned to loiter for most of the rest of her shift. Another man stood at the front desk counter now, answering Sophie's customer-service chirps with monosyllabic murmurs. He wore a jersey, but Esther didn't know anything about teams. She liked the shirt because it seemed almost iridescent.

She stared while emptying the garbage can, studying his shorts, next. They very nearly reached his ankles but they weren't pants, had no taper. Just straight down. Like rectangles. Lego pants. His thin white legs stuck out like popsicle sticks, all two inches that she could see.

He was like one of those popsicles that change color from bottom to top. She smiled as she thought it, then pressed her chin to her chest, concentrating on opening a new garbage bag. But his shoes were a brilliant white and impeccably clean. Esther was impressed. "You can tell a lot about a man based on the way he takes care of his shoes," her dad used to say. She had never once understood what he meant. All she knew was that this guy had to work pretty hard to keep his shoes that clean.

Oblivious to the laughter coming from the small group of guests at the table next to her, Esther sprayed lemon-scented furniture polish on the end table, wiped, saw a streak in her reflection, and wiped again. She looked up when Sophie cleared her throat loudly. The young girl jerked her neck toward the entrance to the front desk.

That's right, Esther reminded herself. No spritzing when the guests are right there. She grabbed her cleaning caddy and headed toward Sophie. The phone rang.

"Thank you for choosing the Westward Inn, you've reached Sophie. To whom may I direct your call?"

The greeting, repeated dozens of times each night, and sometimes five times in three minutes, became a nuanced drawl, a blur of syllables that left callers stammering, "I'm sorry, what…?"

Sophie jotted down a note in the log book as Esther approached. "Mrs. Rose just called down. She's having trouble with her remote." She opened a drawer and retrieved a worn, folded paper. "Here's the programming guide. You think you can help her? I'd do it myself, but don't want to leave the desk in case any other guests show up." She smiled at Esther and rolled her eyes. "Let me know if she found her credit card, will you?"

Esther knew that Sophie's reluctance to leave the front desk had more to do with her television schedule than with guest check-ins. Even while running her reports and interacting with guests, the girl was always a little too eager to return to her TV show or her game of computer solitaire. She once told Esther that she often she played cards for the entire eight-hour shift. But Sophie was so much nicer than the last girl who had worked the front desk evening shift that Esther didn't mind running extra errands.

She took the programming guide Sophie offered her, even though she knew her way around the hotel remote controls pretty well. The Westward Inn was the red-headed stepsister to the behemoth, 400-room hotel next door, which meant they could only get maintenance if and when Larry had fixed all of the snares at the Renault. They had learned how to manage a lot of things on their own.

Mrs. Rose's room was peculiar. All of the rooms were virtually identical, as was to be expected. Esther knew the variations of each one, of course: room 113 had a coffee stain on the carpet in front of the bathroom; 227 had the towel rung installed upside-down. The people and things who moved through the rooms were different. Laptops and pressed suits in the closets, wet bathing suits and discarded fruit-snack bags, beer cans and blackened brillo-pads.

Mrs. Rose preferred the "oddball" room, 200. It had a single bed in it, but instead of a king it was a double. Amazingly, Esther always thought, potential guests scoffed. A double? Just one double bed? They demanded a reduced rate. The front desk could only ever rent it out to desperate room-seekers when the hotel was nearly sold out. For Mrs. Rose, though, it was perfect. She loved it, and always requested it. Sophie would tease, "As long as it's available." Of course it would be.

"Oh, hello there!" Mrs. Rose seemed surprised, maybe even bothered, that someone was at her door, even if she had just phoned the desk for help. "Come on in."

Esther had the distinct sense, walking through the door, that she had entered Mrs. Rose's living room. The chairs and pillows were covered with cream-colored, lace tea-towels that the woman must have stowed in her giant bag. The ice bucket was already filled, and arranged neatly on the desk with a bottle of Grand Maurnier and a scotch glass. She'd set the glass— which wasn't from the hotel—on a tile coaster, also brought from home.

Mrs. Rose indicated the remote on the bed and shrugged. "It's not working."

Without completing the obligatory array of programming buttons, Esther knew the trouble was with the batteries. The indicator light was dead. "Just a moment, Mrs. Rose. I'll get some fresh batteries. That should take care of it."

Esther stepped into the hall and consulted the clipboard she kept on her at all times while on shift. The front desk printed their reports and checklists twice per shift and the housekeepers annotated them to indicate the status of each room in the hotel.

Room 204, just two doors down, was out of order. Trouble with the AC unit. She could switch out the batteries and get them to Mrs. Rose post haste. Her universal keycard ran green and she opened the door.

The first thing she felt was the sweltering heat, but her confusion grew when she saw the unmade beds, the mess of detritus on the counter—coffee stirrers and shredded sweetener packets. A wave of adrenaline accompanied her involuntary yelp, "Housekeeping!" when the two men shot up from their seated positions, one from the bed and one from the chair by the window.

"Hi! Hi, hey…" the one on the bed said, his hands raised as if her clipboard were a weapon. Her gaze might as well have been.

The man took a few cautious steps forward and she saw the other guy put his hand toward his hip, reaching for—she let out a small squeak when she recognized the outline of a gun.

"I'm sorry." She saw the remote on the bed and pointed. "I just…I needed batteries." She trailed off, looking about the room and trying to catch her breath. "I thought this room was out of order."

The one closer to her, who had been on the bed, fluffed his sleeveless flannel shirt against his chest a few times. "It is. No air conditioning." His blond hair was darkened from sweat and he flashed her a smile. "Are you Esther?"

Her eyes widened. Were they after her? What had she done wrong?

Esther pointed toward the door with an impotent finger. "I'll just…I'm sorry to have…" She turned abruptly, opening the door. She didn't stop running until she was behind the front desk.

An episode of *Friends* was playing on the lobby television and Sophie was staring blankly at the computer screen, where stacks of hearts and spades were bounding triumphantly across the screen in celebration of another successful game of solitaire.

She hardly looked up when Esther came bounding down the stairs. "What the hell happened to you?"

Esther was panting. "Men…there's two men…room 204…"

That got Sophie's attention. Her eyes bulged and her jaw dropped. "Oh my god, Esther. I was about to tell you and then—"

"Who the hell are they? How do they know my name?"

Sophie planted her hands on the desk, shaking her head. "I'm sorry, Esther. I was about to tell you when Mrs. Rose called down about her remote. I didn't think—"

"You knew about this?" Esther was still flattened against the door to the front desk.

"Esther. Esther, please…let me explain." Sophie gave a simpering smile.

"It's my fault, honestly."

Esther nearly hit the floor when the man's baritone voice interrupted them. The dark-haired one who had been sitting by the window in room 204 was standing there at the counter. He glanced at the cards on Sophie's computer screen. "Do you have a minute?"

Sophie straightened her shoulders, standing at attention, and Esther peeled herself away from the door, letting one last shiver of adrenaline race through her body before she opened it and let the man in.

His long legs cleared the entrance in a single stride, and he stood before them like an announcement. "Hello, Sophie." He turned to Esther and extended a hand. "Detective Greg Putnam. I'm sorry we scared you."

Esther gave him a grimace of a smile but didn't shake his hand. Greg didn't seem surprised by this and he indicated the stairwell with a nod of his head. "My partner Ben is up in the room. We can't both leave at the same time if we're going to do the job."

Sophie was nodding solemnly, staring at Greg. "It's such important work. Anything we can do to help..."

Esther frowned, her eyes bouncing from Sophie to Greg. She'd never had a boyfriend, but she'd had her fair share of illicit crushes. The tension here was palpable. And infuriating.

Greg shut the front desk door behind him. With the door closed, he towered over both of them. He crossed his arms and spoke in a low voice. "There's a very dangerous and influential individual staying at this little hotel."

"Wait, he's dangerous?" Sophie gasped.

"Yes." Greg looked from Sophie to Esther. "The guy in room 203 is one of the biggest coke dealers in the city. We're staying across the hall to keep tabs on his movements." He let out a big breath and continued. "Really, we need you to be on the lookout. Hotels are a huge resource to traffickers, especially with this city being such a huge Midwestern traffic stop. You have to look out for people who pay in cash, only stay for one night, don't have bags with them—"

He was listing the qualifying suspicions when Esther spoke up. "That's...about half of our clientele."

Greg exhaled again, adding an affirming nod. "You're absolutely right." He drew himself taller. "But you know, you need to be on the lookout for people who just don't seem right. Suspicious people."

Sophie leaned in toward Greg, speaking in a conspiratorial whisper. "He stopped by the desk just a little bit ago. Said he wanted a menu for the restaurant next door. Esther, he's the guy who was standing up here earlier, remember? Tall guy, football jersey? His name is Charlie Mills."

"Good, that's good." Greg nodded approvingly and Sophie beamed. "We're going to need any updates on his movement, Sophie. This city is a bigger hub than you'd think, and this guy is more than a big fish." He turned to Esther. "And you're our point person in housekeeping. We need to keep this operation close. Got it?"

Esther stared, digesting this new information. She didn't suppose her newly-appointed status came with a pay raise. She shrugged. "Well, sure. But if he's dangerous, I mean, what if I have to go into his room?"

"All's we need is for you guys to tell us about his movement, okay? We've spoken to management next door and everything is under control. There's no indication that he's any threat to anyone here in the building. "

"You got it, Greg." Sophie smiled and blinked her eyelids just a little too slowly. "Just let me know if there's anything we can do to help."

"Actually, there is." Greg returned the smile. "Do you have any more coffee packets?"

***

Esther was a few minutes late the next morning on account of the bus, and so she started the shift with compensatory gusto, casting occasional glances at Janelle, the front desk girl, to make sure she saw her going the extra mile. Janelle didn't seem to notice.

"A pad of butter? Don't get up, Mr. Owsinksi. I'll get it." Esther tried to sound cheerful.

The old regular grunted at his paper and sipped his coffee without looking up.

Esther was swabbing waffle slop from the counter when Mrs. Rose approached the coffee machine. "Good morning, Mrs. Rose."

The older woman started, jostling her coffee, then appeared to regain her senses with an unsure smile. "Oh, good morning, dear."

"Were you able to watch *SVU* after I got you those batteries for your remote?" The waffle mess gone, Esther tossed a few empty sugar packets into the trash and used her damp towel to wipe away a few errant crystals.

Coffee creamer dribbled down Mrs. Roses's styrofoam cup and she wiped it with the tissue in her hand. "Oh, yes. I watched three episodes before I fell asleep on my crossword puzzle. An eight-letter word for—"

She stopped, mid-sentence, and Esther followed her line of sight to the man standing at the front desk counter. Janelle was nodding at him with a practiced, polite face as he towered over her. His voice carried over the breakfast area.

"Yeah, okay. And how much is her room each stay?"

Janelle looked around, looking unsure of herself. She said something else before she picked up the phone and started dialing.

"Benjamin!" Mrs. Rose set her coffee cup down on the nearest table, where it splashed onto the mottled formica, and walked toward the man with her arms extended. "I'm so glad you made it.

"Mom, hi." Benjamin accepted his mother's embrace, but only returned it with a noncommittal squeeze of her elbows. He looked around the room like an embarrassed middle-schooler. Esther studied him as she took a quick dab at the spilled coffee under Mrs. Roses's cup. His strawberry-blond hair glistened with hairgel, but the rest of him was wrinkled and nondescript, down to his graying, untied tennis shoes.

"Mom, I stayed at the apartment last night," he said, taking a seat at the table. "I don't think there's anything going on there."

"Are you hungry, Benjamin? I don't think they'd mind if you joined me for a danish." Mrs. Rose tittered around the table, indicating the display case of pastries and reaching for some napkins.

"They better not mind, Mom. Not with the money you spend here." His voice was menacing.

Mrs. Rose faltered, then frowned. "Now, Benjamin, come on. Keep your voice down. I really like the people here." She set a napkin down in front of him. "Oh, did you know Mr. Price is going to stay here while he has work done on his house? I told him to call—"

"Mom. I need you to listen to me." Benjamin balled the napkin in his hand. "I stayed in your apartment last night. There aren't any raccoons. I didn't hear anything or see anything. Mr. Winslow is getting tired of you complaining about it."

Mrs. Rose sipped her coffee with both hands and looked up at her son over the rim of the cup. "I'm not crazy, Benny. They scuffle through the walls. I'm worried about the wiring!"

Benjamin slammed the wrinkled napkin down on the table. Mrs. Rose jumped. Esther did, too, though she continued wiping the leaves on the artificial tree in front of the window, trying to look casual. She turned toward the front desk, where Janelle was casting furtive glances at Mrs. Rose's table while pretending to look at a report. Mr. Owsinski, seated at the table next to Mrs. Rose, shuffled his newspaper and cleared his throat.

"Mom, we've talked about this. You can't keep staying in a hotel. Sarah and I can't afford to pay for this. You need to talk to Doctor Haberforth again." Benjamin was trying to speak quietly, but he had one of those voices that rang out, especially with the lobby's acoustics.

Mrs. Rose made a couple of noises in her throat, shaking her head in sharp little twitches. She gripped her coffee in her hands. "No, Benjamin. I don't think you understand. It's not just me. The neighbor…the neighbor says…"

The ring of the front desk phone jolted the air, and Janelle lifted it immediately in a relieved panic, even though training told them to let it ring twice. "Thank you for choosing the Westward Inn, you've reached Janelle. To whom may I direct your call?"

Mr. Owsinski, the old regular, stood abruptly and gathered his things. He threw his plate in the trash can and sent quick glances around the lobby as he folded his newspaper. Then down the stairs came Charlie Mills, the man from 203, wearing a different-colored jersey this morning with the same long shorts, muttering monosyllabic phrases into the cellphone on his ear. He gave a head-nod in greeting to the lobby in general.

Benjamin leaned forward and whispered, though his voice still carried through the room enough that Charlie looked back at him, cellphone squeezed between neck and shoulder, standing in front of the cereal selection.

"Goddammit, Mom, the apartment next to you has been empty for months. Winslow says he can't get anyone to stay on that floor because you're constantly prattling around, up and down the hall! We can't keep doing this!"

"I'm not doing *anything,* Benjamin! You leave me alone!" Mrs. Rose jumped up, the jolt of her motion sending the contents of her coffee into the air. The occupants of the lobby all stopped, each giving up the façade of minding their own business, and watched as the arc of brown liquid rounded and then collapsed, splashing onto the table, the chair, the floor, Mr. Owsinki.

"God DAMN it!" The old man bellowed. His hands flew up in instinctive outrage, the pages of his paper cascading down in sheaths of black and gray.

Esther lurched forward, involuntarily; her damp rag extended. Mr. Owsinki backed away from her, slapping the hot coffee away from his shirt. Droplets landed in small splashes and Mrs. Rose, bringing her hands to her face, added a few tears to the downpour.

Benjamin was standing, too, his arms frozen to his sides. His cheeks wobbled as his chin worked to find words. "I'm so sorry, sir. Please, let me take care of the laundry bill, I—"

Mr. Owsinski threw his hands down in disgust and stalked toward the hallway door, flinging it open and snarling as he disappeared toward the guest rooms.

Esther marched to the utility room for the mop and winced as its squeaking wheels cut through the uneasy silence in the lobby. Janelle clicked distractedly on her computer, holding the phone with her other hand; Charlie was stirring his coffee slowly, not letting the stirrer hit the sides. Mrs. Rose stood rooted to the spot.

Benjamin blinked stupidly for a moment before he shook his head. "I can't deal with this. I gotta get outta here."

"Ben, wait!" Mrs. Rose called.

Her son stalked out of the lobby and through the front door. "I'll call you later, Mom!" He didn't look back.

Mrs. Rose crumpled into her chair, covering her face with her hands. Esther's mop sloshed quietly on the tiled floor, her eyes glued to her work, and at the front desk, two separate lines were ringing. Charlie stared at his coffee.

"Thank you for choosing the Westward Inn, you've reached Janelle. Can you please hold for a moment?"

Mrs. Rose's shoulders bounced slightly from the force of silent sobs as Charles approached her. "Excuse me, ma'am?" Her head snapped up, and she looked slightly alarmed before her expression gave way to one of general, resigned confusion.

"We met at the ice machine last night, remember?" Charlie put his hand on his chest. "Chaz."

Mrs. Rose nodded with a sniff and dabbed at her nose with a napkin.

"Can I get you another cup of coffee? You dropped yours."

"No, no..." Her voice was soft and the syllables sounded far away, like she was answering a different question. She looked down at the mess Esther was cleaning up and her face clouded. "Oh, Mira, you klutz! Always getting into some mess or another."

Charlie smiled and put a hand on her shoulder. "I'm on my way back upstairs. Can I walk you to your room?"

The grayed mop water sloshed against the sides while Esther watched the two guests walking up the stairs, side by side. When they reached the landing, Charlie held the door for her. He said something Esther couldn't hear and it made Mrs. Rose laugh. For all of Detective Greg's warnings the night before, the man she had just watched in the lobby certainly didn't seem dangerous.

"That was something, wasn't it?"

Janelle's voice jerked Esther back to the lobby. She looked around. All the guests had gone and it was 10 am, time to put up breakfast. She started gathering trays of iced yogurt and fruit and replied, "I'm not entirely certain what just happened."

Once she had cleared the breakfast center, wiped down the counters, tables, and chairs, and mopped the lobby floor in its entirely, Esther packed her housekeeping cart and grabbed her clipboard from the front desk. Twenty-two checkouts, eighteen stayovers, and nine do-not-disturbs. She split the rooms between the girls who had shown up that day, allocating the second-floor north wing for herself.

She wanted to check on Mrs. Rose, and also knew that the detectives a few doors down were her responsibility. And room 203.

Eyeing her chart when she'd reached her set of rooms, Esther was disappointed and surprised to find that Mrs. Rose was on the do-not-disturb list. That was new. The scene during breakfast must have really shaken the poor woman.

She finished cleaning room 202, where Esther could still smell a tinge of the woman's perfume. Elizabeth and James, Nirvana Black. She knew this because when she'd emptied the bathroom wastebasket, the little vial of cologne spilled out. After looking around to make sure no one was watching, she'd pocketed the discarded perfume sample. Outside of Charlie's room, she paused to listen. His voice undulated with the murmur of the television, likely on his cellphone again.

Esther shrugged inwardly, squeaking her cart down to 204. She wouldn't have anything to report. She knocked. No answer. "Housekeeping!" She knocked again. Nothing. She swiped her keycard and opened the door, finding a room littered with questionable magazines, scattered coffee grounds, and a few discarded beer cans. The bedding on both mattresses was pulled back and the contents of a fast food bag were strewn across one of the beds. *They're not really even guests,* Esther thought to herself. An image of the man soaking in Sophie's adulterating smile crossed her mind. *They're taking advantage of our hospitality.*

She turned on her heel and walked out of the room, too furious to clean up the mess these men hadn't paid to make. A rage rose up in her, one she'd never really known before, and she marched to the front desk.

"They're not even there!" she complained to Janelle, who had been briefed on the situation by the log book and a few careful calls from management next door. "The room they're not paying for is filthy, and they're not even watching this man they claim is such a danger to society!"

Janelle blew a wisp of hair from her face and shrugged without looking up from the fingernail she was filing. "They called this morning. Said they probably wouldn't be in today because their supervisor won't file for the overtime."

Esther tried to calm down. There were more rooms to clean, she reminded herself. But this really wicked her wicket, as her mother would say.

"Esther, it's fine." Janelle had stopped filing her nails and was staring at her. "They're still patrolling the place. They asked us to keep tabs on when he comes and goes."

"So, on top of my job I have to do theirs? I guess I'll start by cleaning the room they didn't even pay for!"

Janelle was watching Esther in wide-eyed fascination. She'd never seen the mousy girl express an opinion, forget releasing a diatribe. "Oh, I don't know. I think it's kind of exciting. I get to play—OH, *hello Mr. Mills!"*

The abrupt volume change in Janelle's voice startled Esther. She whipped her head toward the hall door and saw Charlie walking toward the front desk. His steps were slow as he was thumbing through his wallet while he walked. Janelle stood alert, wiggling the computer mouse on the desk to wake up the computer. "How can I help you?"

His eyes darted beneath the brim of his ball cap, looking from Janelle to Esther. "Yeah, uhm, that was crazy stuff down here a little bit ago, wasn't it?"

Janelle opened her eyes wider in question. "I'm sorry…?"

"You know, with that dude and his moms. That poor lady with the coffee."

Janelle gave an exaggerated nod. He hadn't looked at Esther since first walking to the desk, and she took this opportunity to fade into the back office. She wiped down the phones and walkie-talkies, absently, while she listened.

"Yeah, hey. I don't know what's going on with all that and I don't know if this is allowed, but she seemed pretty worked up about money. Telling me her son won't pay for her to stay here." He sniffed and cocked his head. "I don't know. I don't know what they got going on but I'm like, hey, she kinda reminds me of my moms, and if she wants to stay here sometimes, like she says, well...I don't know if I'm allowed to, but I wanna pay for her to stay here a coupla nights. Like, she gets a couple nights on me."

Esther glanced at the back of Janelle's head. The girl was frozen for a moment and Esther couldn't see her face.

"I..."

He started talking again, his voice low but rapid. He sounded embarrassed. "I don't know. I don't want to sound crazy but like I said, she just remind me of some people I know, and I want to do something nice. She seems like someone who could use someone being nice to her."

Janelle reanimated, and she started clicking and typing on the computer. Her voice was higher-pitched than usual when she spoke. "It's no problem at all, Mr. Mills. People pay for people's rooms all the time. That's really nice of you. She really is such a sweetheart, too."

Charlie nodded but didn't say anything. He tapped his wallet on the counter.

"So, will you use a credit card?" Janelle asked.

Esther frowned. She knew that no one was going to leave a credit card on file for a perfect stranger, let alone this guy. She straightened up, realizing what Janelle was trying to do. "Try to get a credit card," the cop had said. "Anything we can get a trail on." Janelle, the gumshoe.

Esther exhaled quietly when Charlie said simply, "Nah, sorry. I got bad credit. Cash okay?"

Janelle's shoulders, which had been hitched up just a tiny bit higher than usual, sank down like something in her had deflated. *There go her chances of entering detective school,* Esther thought.

"Perfectly okay, sir. Let me get this set up and get you a total." Her ponytail quivered as she made the tiny motions of clicking and typing, observing the screen.

"Yeah, and uh, how bout that other dude, you know the guy with the shirt?"

Janelle stopped moving, her ponytail slowing. Esther looked down to the floor, thinking.

"I'm sorry?" Janelle said.

"The dude who was pissed about the coffee on his clothes. Ain't no thing. Tell him to put it in the laundry and the hotel gets the bill. I'll pay."

Janelle didn't move. She just stared.

Charlie pulled out several crisp twenty-dollar bills from his wallet. "I know I get mad when somebody spill something on me. But I don't want no bad blood between this lady and her son, or this other dude. It ain't cool. She's such a nice lady."

Janelle's head was bobbing up and down in another set of nods. "Certainly, sir. I'll send him a message right away." She wrote a few notes down on a sheet of paper. "That's very kind of you."

Esther exited the front office without looking at either of them and made a beeline for the stairs, returning to where she'd left her cart in the hallway. She couldn't make sense of what she had just witnessed. The white noise of the vacuum would help her sort it out. She started picking up the trash in 204,

determined to get the room squared away. The cops wouldn't
be coming back, she would make certain of it.

She had started on the bathroom when she heard the sound
of footsteps. Charlie was padding down the carpeted hallway in
those clean, white tennis shoes of his. He paused in front of his
door, fumbling with the keycard, and Esther stepped into the
hall, idly arranging things on her cart.

"They're watching you." She didn't look at him when she
spoke, but she felt him freeze in place. Slowly, like a
mechanical clock, she turned her neck in increments to meet his
gaze. He was staring at her, his pale blue eyes hard.

"Say what now?" His mouth barely moved.

Esther snapped back into motion and grabbed a stack of
towels. The terrycloth tickled her chin when she spoke again,
drawing out every syllable. "They are watching you. You need
to leave." She flicked a glance in his direction before walking
back into 204. His eyes were still on her, softer now, and doing
a lot of quick calculations.

Esther didn't know if he believed her or if he would listen
to her. She wasn't sure why she'd even spoken up. It just didn't
seem fair. She set the towels on the rack and threw the soiled
ones against the wall. Why the towels had been used in the first
place, she thought bitterly. She'd have to treat this room like a
check-out, full service. She wiped down the sink and avoided
eye contact with her reflection when she cleared a few
fingerprints from the mirror. The toilet would need cleaned, she
supposed.

She stepped back to her cart to retrieve the toilet cleaner and
wand, casting a casual glance up and down the hall as she did.
she was just in time to see Charlie Mills opening the door to the

stairwell. He turned slightly and caught sight of her. He lifted his chin sharply, acknowledging her, then walked away.

Reaching for the things she needed, she froze. Her clipboard had been moved. It laid askew on top of the towels. She frowned. That wasn't where she had left it. She took it in her hands and examined it then gasped, startled, when crisp pieces of paper fluttered to the floor. Green pieces of paper.

She gathered the bills and stuffed them in her the pocket of her uniform shirt, looking up and down the hall as she did so. She stole back into 204's bathroom, this time shutting the room door behind her and locking it. When she pulled out all of the bills and counted them, her eyes welled with tears. He had given her two thousand dollars.

Esther ran to the window and pulled aside the curtain. Rattling the windows with his bass as he passed, Charlie Mills used his turn signal to exit the parking lot onto the busy street.

Lucrative Therapy

anielle slammed the drawer shut. The money in the envelope matched the money on the slip, so Doctor Short should be happy. She'd even written it out line by line—cash, credit, check (she couldn't believe he still took checks), and insurance payments.

It wasn't rocket science but he'd hovered over her shoulder for the first week she handled the money. The man had trust issues, even if she was his niece. Fair enough, considering there was an extra twenty-dollar bill lining her pocket that evening.

Her dad had insisted she got a job at the office. "It's going to look great on your college applications," he'd hollered after her on her way in to the interview. Yes, having her dad sit in the parking lot waiting for her looked great, especially yelling out encouragements. And yes, Doctor Short, her uncle, had insisted on the formality. She exerted effort, throughout the entire interrogation, to not roll her eyes, and to not blurt out, "I'm just here to make my dad happy and get out of the house and maybe make some spending money in the meantime!"

Uncle—*Doctor* Short had made notes on his legal pad and then stood up to shake her hand, telling her she'd start Monday at the standard minimum wage. So much for spending money. It seemed a steep price—or whatever the opposite of that was— for handling secure medical information, HIPPA and all of the that. She had so many acronyms to memorize, and she hated all of it.

Danielle looked up when the vacuum cleaner cut off at the end of the hall and she exhaled silently with relief she hadn't known she needed. The renewed quiet soaked into the air. "You about finished up?" she asked.

A mangy-looking woman peeked her head out of the staff breakroom. "Yeah, this is always the last room."

Danielle mimicked the words to herself as she gathered her coat and purse. She was tired of the other employees lording "the process" over her head. Everything had a way it was done, an order, and there was a reason for each step. If that were the case, Danielle thought darkly, then why the hell did that lady have a job here? To pick up odds and ends? She jiggled her keys impatiently and Esther, who had wound up the extension cord and put the vacuum cleaner away, made her way to the front counter, her old Carhartt coat under her arm.

"I hope you had a good week, Danielle. See you Monday!" Esther turned and walked out the front door.

Danielle forced a smile at her co-worker, which faded the second the other's back had turned. No, not co-worker. An underling, even if Danielle had only been there a few weeks. That woman—that kind of woman—would always be an underling to Danielle. Esther might have seniority because she'd been there for over five years, but it was a pity hire and everyone knew it. Danielle was the boss's niece and set on college, where she'd study pharmacy and prescribe drugs like a real medical practitioner, not like these physical therapy sops.

The truth was, the office training hadn't been horrible. The gig here might not be so bad, even if she'd never let her parents know she thought that. It was definitely better than teaching swimming classes at the Y. Those snot-nosed, screaming kids made her skin crawl. The infuriating thing was her parents' insistence that she have a job. She didn't need the money. Her parents were just hell-bent on instilling in her some sense of work ethic.

"We're always going to provide for you, honey," Mom had cooed at her. The woman hadn't had a job in decades. Dad chimed in, "We just want you to know what it is to, you know, have a job. We don't want you to be one of those entitled kids."

Apparently neither one of them had picked up on the irony that Daddy had gone running to his older brother when things got out of hand with Danielle at the Y. She had yelled at one of the little kids and got fired when his parents filed a complaint. Her dad was convinced this office job would be the thing that motivated her, got her in line.

She patted the extra twenty-dollar bill in her pocket before locking up the office. Danielle always had an aptitude for math, her accountant father said.

***

The next week brought more headaches. They were expecting several new patients on top of their already-bursting schedule, and then, to make matters worse, Uncle Don told Danielle that, from here on out, she would only be able to take a thirty-minute lunch and it would be her job to open up the office for the afternoon patients.

"What about Esther?" She protested. "Isn't that like, the whole point of her being here?"

Uncle Don sighed and looked down, his hands on the back of his hips and accentuating his paunch. It was the stance he took when he disapproved of something, like when an insurance company denied further treatment for a patient who needed it, or when she'd pushed her older cousin Marla into the pool a few summers ago. "It's simple, Danny. Esther opens up in the morning. She walks here, and I think it's best she has a bit longer of a break at lunch now that you're here. That's final." He turned and walked into his office, clicking on his dictation machine.

Danielle stomped to the laundry room, taking care to peek in on the staff lounge on her way there. Esther was standing, stock-still, in front of the refrigerator. It was obvious she'd been listening. Indignant rage boiled over and Danielle knocked over one of the rehab weights. Predictably, Esther jumped about three feet in the air and something fell to the floor with a clatter. She scrambled to the floor, snatching up a tiny tin box of mints and stuffing it in her pocket.

Doctor Short poked his head out of his office, dictation microphone at his chin. "Everything okay?"

"Everything's good, Uncle Don! Just dropped a weight!" Danielle smiled and pointed to the laundry room, where she was headed.

He frowned slightly but nodded and went back into his office. Danielle caught Esther's eyes when she turned round and glowered at her. "He'll want that picked up," she said. She had a lighter step as she headed to fold the pile of gowns in the dryer.

Her uncle refused to invest in paper gowns. Too many patients came in and out of here, he said, and it was bad for the environment. They washed and reused the same decades-old, threadbare gowns and towels every day. They were warm and irresistibly soft coming out of the dryer, though. After Danielle had folded the hand towels in preparation for the afternoon shift, she looked down the hall. Uncle Don had stepped out to grab his lunch at the Mediterranean place next door, like he did every day.

Knowing she had at least twenty minutes before the front door chime would alert her, she crawled up onto the exam table they used to fold clothes and nestled into the pile of warm linens. It was like heaven. If she was only getting thirty minutes of breaktime between loads of patients, she knew she needed to maximize her relaxation.

***

Her first reaction, on waking, was panic. Had she missed the door chime? Were patients already in the waiting room, impatient to start their therapies? Fury replaced fear when she realized the source of her sleep's disruption.

"You...shouldn't be sleeping in the clean gowns." Esther stood before her, in her hand the XX-large down that Danielle had used to cover herself with. Her voice had a stout edge to it, and it surprised both of them.

Danielle had been caught red-handed, and her mind raced. Would Esther tell her uncle? "I'm sorry. You're—you're right." She yawned and gave a dramatic stretch. "I'm just so tired. I've been up all night studying for entrance exams. This schedule is killing me."

Esther nodded, folding the gown carefully on the table. "I understand. My mom always worked me really hard." She grabbed another gown from the pile, tugging it gently out from underneath Danielle's elbow. "Tell you what. I can fold the clothes from the morning patients during my lunch break. That way you get more rest."

Danielle's eyes widened. "Really? You'd do that?"

Esther brushed her coarse bangs away from her face and shrugged, folding another gown. Danielle saw that she wasn't really that old, probably only a few years older than she was. It made the pasty-skinned girl seem even more pathetic.

"You're a real pal, Esther! Thank you!" Danielle hopped off the table and made for the door. When she turned to say something else, she saw that Ester's cheeks had reddened. "You're really good at this stuff. So much better than me." At this, Esther flushed even more darkly, and Danielle nearly skipped away, chuckling to herself.

***

Elicia, the gal who handled most of the patient therapies, was getting married soon and wouldn't be as available to run the patient therapies. As such, Doctor Short asked Danielle to take on some training in addition to her work at the front desk. As she did with most things, she responded begrudgingly.

Applying the TENS pads wasn't so bad. The patient was lying face down on a table, unable to see Danielle roll her eyes at them, their voice muffled. She'd wet the pads, stick them on where the patient needed them, pump up the juice, then leave the room. That was always the best part.

For ultrasound therapy, though, she had to stay in the room with the patient. Usually for a full ten minutes. She stood there, looking longingly at the door, while making small talk about the weather, weekend plans, gardening, school, family…barf. Danielle did her best to sound interested, or at least not to roll her eyes. Her favorite patients were the ones who preferred she administer the therapy in silence. Only slightly better were the ones who asked her questions about her life.

There was never a bad time for Danielle to talk about herself. She prattled away happily about the university's spring break schedule, the best way to assemble a salad, and her humble plans for redecorating her bedroom. "I'm trying to save money. We can't all shop at Ethan Allen, right? I mean, the rest of us have to shop at Oak Express."

Danielle delighted in discussing the minutiae of her day, and found it a comfort while she was stuck there, staring at the skin on the patient's back. When she had to administer a lumbar therapy, their butt would be almost entirely exposed and she desperately needed things to take her mind off of the scenario at hand.

These ten-minute therapy excursions got her mind working in new ways. After spending several sessions administering ultrasound therapy on a particular patient, for instance, she noticed that on one side of his spine the hair was curly, while on the other side it was straight. She wondered whether it was true that on the opposite side of the earth, cyclones flew in reverse and the drains swirled backward. Would his back hair curl the opposite way in Australia?

She giggled in the staff room about this, while Esther smiled and looked uncomfortable. Esther only rarely took part in patient treatments, though she'd been called upon from time to time as an extra set of hands.

Danielle noticed that although Uncle Don had left the lunch table shaking his head, and Elicia was consumed with reading *Bridal* magazines, Esther was alert and leaning forward, listening to Danielle describe some of the patients' grooming habits, or lack thereof. Her fingernails tapped idly on the tin mintbox she kept in her pocket.

"Can we talk about the moles?" Danielle ribbed Elicia, who rolled her eyes and continued thumbing through her magazine. "Mr. Dennis has this thing on his shoulder that looks like a piece of bubble-gum popped on his skin and just…stayed there. It's all thin and wrinkly and pink."

Elicia glanced up. Apparently, she couldn't resist after all. "I call it Mr. Shoulder Testicle."

Danielle threw her head back, laughing. "Oh my god, I never would have thought of that. Or how about Ed Pisanelli's sticky back-hair?"

She had both of the girls' attention now. Elicia smirked, and Esther set down her bottle of water.

"What do you mean? They stick together?" she asked.

"Exactly that." Danielle took a dainty bite of salad and chewed, relishing the moment. "It's like, a bunch of squiggly back hairs all sticking together but I don't know what's holding them. Like, I wanted to believe it was just some band-aid residue, but I couldn't see that band-aid outline, you know? I think it was just like, legit back funk holding them all in a weird back-hair ponytail."

Esther leaned back, considering this, and Elicia shook her head.

Danielle pounced. "Elicia, you're about to get married. You have to have it in your contract somewhere so that you have to call out your spouse when their back funk congeals into one large, dirty hair cluster."

Elicia threw a tomato at Danielle, and the three girls laughed. Then she added, "Back funk isn't that common, thank god. But do you guys notice…the smell? Like, fermented people smell under the hot packs?"

Esther nodded knowingly and spoke, with a timid, controlled voice, "Even a slight to moderate body odor is multiplied tenfold after we simmer the patient with hot packs for fifteen minutes."

Danielle slammed her hand on the pleather patient bench they used for a lunch table, upsetting the silverware and napkins. She cackled with her mouth full, spraying out bits of shredded cheese from her salad. "I have *categories* of smells!

There's fermented old man, fermented two-pack-a-day smoker—"

"Fermented old lady is different, somehow," Elicia noted, squinting her eyes with mock wisdom.

"And fermented fat person, man or lady!" Danielle erupted at that point, snorting with laughter.

"Oh my god...so many smells." Elicia had thrown aside her magazine and started mimicking patient voices. "'I just mowed the lawn.' And my personal favorite, 'I had a pickle with lunch.'"

"And those weird, 'I can't put my finger on it' odors. Sometimes I go home thinking about them. Lord knows I soak it all up in these scrubs." Danielle spread her hands over her thick waist, shaking her head.

"All I ever smell is Bio-Freeze when I get home." Esther let out a nervous laugh and then spoke again, softly. "So, every person has a different smell coming out of their pores?"

Danielle shot her an annoyed look, though she was still laughing. "Well, duh. That's just how human physiology works. I mean, let's face it. We're all just animals."

Esther shrunk slightly from these words and Elicia cut in. "There are some amazing fragrances, though. Let's be fair."

"Mrs. Hoover. Pantene Pro-V." Danielle stuck her fork in the air to punctuate her point.

Elicia nodded in agreement, then added, "Who's the hot guy who always smells like a bonfire?"

"John Sutton." Esther and Danielle spoke in unison. Danielle guffawed, but Esther blushed.

The three of them laughed until their giggles turned into exaggerated sighs, and they waited on one another to say something funny again. Finally, Danielle took another dig in the air with her fork, doing a Seinfeld impression with her voice. "And what's the deal with the spittle? Where have you ever been in your adult life that you thought it was okay to just drool?"

Elicia laughed, adding, "It is kind of weird. I guess some of them just pass out?"

Danielle didn't skip a beat. "And they don't notice they've left a puddle of spit on the exam table?"

"I clean it up. I have to wipe the rung between the face sheets when the patients drool on it."

The other two girls sobered when Esther said this. It was her job to clean up the rooms once the therapies were complete. Noticing this, the girl tried to add an element of intrigue. "They leave a lot of skin flakes, too."

At this, Danielle stopped poking at her salad, laden with parmesan cheese. "Yup, I'm good. That's enough gross for me in one lunch hour." She stood up, and Elicia joined her, stretching her back as she did so.

Esther watched her coworkers put away their lunches and prepare for the afternoon patients. She didn't want the lively conversation to end on a note she'd soured.

"Edgar Moseman," she said, abruptly. The other two girls turned and gave her the same inquisitive look. She shrugged. "He smells really good."

At this, the two girls burst into fits of laughter, Danielle leaning on the door frame before she set about turning on the therapy machines for the next shift. "Esther, oh my god. You kill me."

"It's your lucky day, girl. He's on the schedule at three today." Elicia giggled and left the room.

Esther hadn't really meant it as a joke.

***

They were swamped that afternoon. Danielle had established a good rhythm, commanding patients to their rooms and getting therapies started, while Elicia sent them on their way with reminder cards for their next appointment. Esther kept the laundry moving, and tidied the rooms after each appointment concluded.

Every time Esther finished cleaning a room, Danielle heard a distinct, tinny "click" before the girl emerged from the room. It had to be that stupid mintbox she carried around. It became Pavlovian, and Danielle knew the next patient could come back once she'd heard the click. Still, she wondered about it. Nobody could consume that many mints in close succession.

At three o'clock, the front door opened and a short man entered the office. Danielle watched with renewed curiosity as he removed his hat, scratched at some dry skin on his forehead and the small amount of greasy-hair stuck to his forehead, then replaced the hat. She was ready with his file when he stepped to the window.

"Mr. Moseman!" She said it a bit louder than necessary. Esther came to a jerking stop in front of the X-ray closet. "We have a room ready for you. Come on back!"

The man raised his eyebrows in surprise. "Moving fast today, huh?" His voice was strangely muffled, like he had an invisible wad of tissues pressed against his face.

Totally Esther's type, Danielle thought to herself. As he walked past the front counter, Danielle paused and inhaled carefully. She recognized it instantly. Old Spice. A smile spread across her face. Definitely Esther's type. "Room three today, Mr. Moseman."

Danielle hurried to finish up her paperwork at the front counter so she could be outside the room three's door once he'd completed his therapies for the day. She couldn't waste an opportunity to tease Esther. Listening closely in the hall, she heard the swish of the laundry bin as Esther threw in the gown and towels, then shuffled around the room. Danielle could picture her, changing the face paper on the table and wiping down the leather, then setting out fresh towels. As dim-witted as the girl was, her movements held a charming rhythm.

Inside the room, it was quiet. Danielle leaned her weight against the door so that when it opened, it was like she exploded into the room. Esther let out a small shriek and clutched her hands to her chest. Danielle was laughing, her hands holding in her round stomach. "Gotta huff that Old Spice, huh?"

Esther's face had gone white, and she was still frozen in her hunched over, startled pose, hands over her heart. Danielle looked at her face for a moment, then said, "Oh, come on, it was just a joke! You look like a dead person!" When Esther still didn't move, Danielle's eyes wandered to where her hands were, and realized the girl was holding something. "What is it?" Immediately, she was more menacing. "Show me what you're holding."

Esther made to move away and Danielle lunged, grabbing at her clutched hands. Esther's grip fell away like paper, and Danielle saw the tiny mint box in her trembling palms. She blinked. "What…? What's the big deal?"

Esther leaned into the wall, her form somehow even smaller and more diminished than usual as Danielle took the box from her. Danielle opened it and frowned, studying its contents.

It looked like something from out of a dustpan. Odd little hairs swirled in with lint fuzz from the carpet, and tiny little soap shavings. "What the hell?" she muttered. She recalled Esther's comment, earlier that day, about patients leaving behind skin flakes. Understanding washed over Danielle and she flung the box away from her. It clattered against the wall and the detritus inside it flickered through the air like an echo, landing on the freshly wiped table and face sheet.

"Tell me..." It was Danielle's turn to tremble. "Tell me that those weren't flakes of skin. You have not been collecting hair and flakes of skin in a little box—" her voice caught in her throat and she gagged.

Doctor Short's voice came over the office loudspeaker, "Therapy in room one, please."

"You wait here." Danielle pointed at Esther, still crumpled against the wall like a pile of laundry. She composed herself and stepped into the hall. "Elicia? Can you get that?" Elicia rolled her eyes and set down the files she'd been arranging.

Danielle turned back into the room, closing the door behind her. She stared at Esther, who threw a glance at her like a beaten dog, her eyes watery. "What is this, Esther? What kind of reject...?" Danielle stopped. She didn't often find herself at a loss for words.

Esther uncurled somewhat, and straightened herself against the wall. She didn't look up. "You can't say anything. I know you've been taking money."

Danielle stiffened and her eyebrows shot up. "No."

"No?" Esther met her gaze. Her eyes had a wild look in them, like a cornered animal.

"No. You don't have the upper hand, here." Danielle spoke in a low, even cadence. Her heart was pounding but she knew, all of her instincts screamed at her, that this girl needed to be gone. Esther had nothing on her. What Esther had done—what she'd been doing—Danielle shook her head. "You need to leave. You know this is worse. Get out. Get your things. Leave."

Neither girl moved for a long time. Esther's eyes darted from the tin box on the floor to Danielle's shoes. Finally, she wiped her eyes, which were streaming with tears. She hoisted herself up from against the wall and shuffled toward the door, which Danielle opened for her. She stopped and looked in Danielle's direction without meeting her eyes, but Danielle held up a hand to silence her before she could speak. "Get out."

Danielle stood at the door and watched Esther gather her coat and scarf from the break room. She moved to the door of the front office and held it open as the girl plodded up the hallway, staring at the floor. Patients in the waiting room looked up, expecting to be called back. They stared as Esther walked past, her face crimson and tear-streaked. She pulled the key to the office from her pocket and made to hand it to Danielle, who didn't move. She set it on the counter instead.

When Esther had opened the front door and the cold January rushed in, Danielle spoke. "Esther?" The girl froze. Her face was still downcast but she turned her head in Danielle's direction. "You're a freak."

In her peripheral vision, Esther saw eyebrows shoot upwards on some of the patients seated in the waiting room, and one of them let out an audible gasp, but she didn't look at any of them. She walked across the parking lot, turning right at the entrance to make her way home.

The cold air bit at the tear tracks on her face until she wiped them away with a mittened hand. She was done crying. Reaching inside her coat pocket, she pulled out another one of the small tin boxes and listened to its contents shuffle against the sides when she shook it. The day wasn't a total loss, after all.

Hardly a Scratch

This was the last thing she needed to deal with today. It couldn't be that hard to make a breakfast sandwich. When the order on the slip says "with egg," why must the sandwich inevitably come wrapped in its greasy sheath *without egg?* The peachfuzz-lipped employee behind the counter—Mike, his nametag said—wiped his nose on the back of his hand and gave a noncommittal holler, "Need sausage breakfast slider with egg, please!"

The incompetence nauseated her. Or maybe it was the eight vapor tons of grease hanging in the air. Why Marty insisted on eating at a place like this boggled her. More than that, it worried her. She knew his health was failing, and if he kept it up with these meals...

Just stop, Cathleen.

She steadied herself on the counter and took a deep breath. In through the nose, out through the mouth. Yoga breaths.

"Sorry for your trouble, ma'am." Nametag Mike nearly had to shout over the noise. She managed a smile, or at least a grimace. Probably more than his surely single, drug-addict mother ever offered him. She'd consider it her good deed for the day.

Somewhere in the kitchen she could hear construction. The sound of the drill reminded her she had a headache.

Probably violating about thirty different health codes, Cathleen thought to herself as she took the bag from him, fresh grease stains already seeping through. Presumably it contained the correct sandwich this time. She held it by a corner and managed a cold smile. "Yes, well, I'm sure I'll be seeing you again soon, Mike."

She grabbed a handful of napkins at the condiment counter, then collided with a bulbous woman who stood staring at the traffic through the front window.

"I'm so sorry," Cathleen said. "I didn't see you there." She really hadn't. When she'd stalked in wielding the bag with the wrong sandwich, the dining room was empty.

The woman turned and simply stared at Cathleen with pink, watery eyes. Or, near Cathleen. It was hard to tell. She didn't seem to be focused on anything. The skin of her face was thin and loose, like it had been stretched and had since gone slack. There was no definable color to it, either. She simply washed away into the dishwater gray sweatshirt she wore.

Cathleen looked over her shoulder, maybe to see if there was something behind her the old woman was staring at. Maybe she just needed to feel like she was doing something. Obviously, there was nothing there. Just an oversized hamburger plastered on the oversized window.

The woman's stare turned into a leer. "Hardly a scratch." She started to snicker, then held a shaking hand up to her face, giggling. Spittle collected at the corners of her mouth and she roared with laughter. Cathleen watched and let out an uncomfortable "Heh," at which point the woman stopped abruptly. Her pale, thin skin pinched into a glare and her eyes blazed. "Hardly a scratch," she whispered. She made a sound that was a cross between a sniff and clearing her throat, then walked toward the counter to place her order.

Cathleen offered a polite laugh and re-shouldered her purse. "Well, uh, have a good one." She lifted her coffee in a weak salute. "See you."

When the woman still didn't move or make any motion whatsoever to acknowledge the executive vice president in front of her, Cathleen gathered her unnerved wits and stalked out of the restaurant. *Whole world's gone mad. Or just stupid.*

***

Walking through the lobby, Cathleen made a mental note of necklines and skirt lengths. Marty was holding interviews today, and if he wasn't careful, he was going to wind up with a lawsuit.

She had to wait to be buzzed in. New office protocol. The building was expanding and the new neighbors were building some sort of medical suite. She'd seen construction workers and medical staff alike wandering through the community break rooms.

Jacey, the flustered girl at the front desk, managed to open the door only after Cathleen had buzzed it twice. "Sorry, I was—"

Cathleen's cold, raised eyebrow cut her off and Jacey shrunk behind her computer until the older woman had reached the boss's office.

"Am I allowed to promote you twice?" Marty said when Cathleen handed him the grease-stained paper bag. His oxygen canister greeted her with its familiar click and whistle.

"Only if I get another raise." Cathleen set her purse down and started taking off her gloves. "Marty, did your ad say that the candidate needed to be a teenager? I have hemorrhoids older than some of those girls out there. And once we're done with this, we're going to need to do something about that useless creature at the front desk."

The old man just waved a hand. He was holding the sandwich in the other and his mouth was full.

"You planning to get started on them?" She didn't know why she bothered asking.

Marty swallowed hard then grinned at her. "I double booked—*that girl up there*—double booked me. I'm due to meet Mr. Hildebrandt and…"

"Just stop." Cathleen rolled her eyes.

He waved again and said, "Don't worry. I'll give you another promotion."

"Another promotion and I'm going to make you my assistant!"

Marty took another mouthful of sandwich and used his waving hand to give a thumbs-up, then pointed to a stack of files on his desk. Cathleen grabbed them and started thumbing through them on the way to her adjoining office.

So, who was the ideal candidate?

***

The interviews went as well as Cathleen could hope for with a wall-to-wall hiring fiasco. It was the only way Marty did things—the most difficult and inconvenient way possible. She'd been hired in the same way, sort of. She'd hardly gotten through the interview before she was in a trial run. Two of the office assistants had quit and the interviewer, obviously overwhelmed, had to take calls while he was asking her the typical "Where do you see yourself in five years" crap. Finally, when a third line started ringing, he asked if she didn't mind picking it up.

That was nearly fifteen years ago. Since then, Cathleen had completely taken over the run of the office. She had streamlined every process, created templates for every communique, oral and written; she'd created the operation. It worked so well that Marty entrusted every part of the process to her, so long as his name was on the marquee.

She and Marty saw eye to eye on a lot of things. When she'd caught the budgeting snafu, the way the Horster account had been overcharged, Marty brought her into a line of thinking she easily understood—more money in her pocket. For several years, she had simply turned a blind eye, until she found out there was more in it for her if she helped with the numbers. They never got greedy, really, just enough for...well, Marty liked to call it a "gratuity."

Clearly, she thought, watching another pair of knees strut out of her office, she was going to have to revisit the conversation where they delineated candidate expectations. The first five interviews offered maybe one potential employee. Cathleen had little hope for the last one of the day.

She checked the file in front of her as a smartly dressed woman walked into the room—modestly dressed, Cathleen noticed with relief. Plaid pants with a gray blazer over a maroon turtleneck. Not the typical "interview suit" option, but it looked sharp, even if the blazer was a bit faded. "Heather?"

"Yes ma'am. Heather Conzen. It's nice to meet you." The woman had a firm handshake, too. Cathleen dared to hope.

Mrs. Conzen had done her homework. She breezed through the preliminary "what would you do" scenario questions, and seemed to know the job requirements and the flavor of the company without Cathleen having to offer much explanation.

This was going to work out quite nicely, Cathleen thought. She stood up to retrieve her clipboard from her desk.

"Your resume has some really interesting items listed under your previous employer...that was Synergy Corp, correct? You strike me as someone who—" *Ouch.* Walking back to her desk, Cathleen knocked her knee against the mobile cart that stupid intern Jacey must have parked there.

She tried really hard not to swear and held up her finger to indicate she would need a minute. With a long exhale she smiled and straightened herself, looking again for the clipboard she'd set down earlier. "Sorry about that."

Mrs. Conzen waved her off. "Oh please, don't apologize. Though I suspect in a place like this, you can't let them see you falter. Not even for a second."

"Excuse me?"

The interview had been going well—so well it almost seemed scripted, Cathleen thought to herself—but what Mrs. Conzen just said was inappropriately presumptuous and borderline contemptuous. Cathleen didn't take well to people overstepping their bounds.

But overstep this interviewee had. And then she had the nerve to stand up and take a step closer, even. She leaned closer toward Cathleen, who bristled, and gave a stage whisper, "Hardly a scratch, right?"

Cathleen felt her hand jerk, but she didn't drop the clipboard she'd located. Very aware of the pacing of the turn of her neck, she turned to face Mrs. Heather Conzen.

The woman looked taller, somehow, and more filled out around the midsection. The gray blazer Cathleen had admired when she first came in had somehow changed. It was a blander gray, if that were possible, somehow nondescript, like a white t-shirt that had mixed too often with darker laundry and finally resulted in a watery, charcoal color. Mrs. Conzen's ashen face wasn't a far shade off, now that she was standing closer. Standing closer and looking at Cathleen, but not quite focused on her.

"Is there something wrong, Cathleen?" the woman asked. It definitely wasn't Mrs. Conzen anymore. Her face looked like it didn't have enough skin to cover it, and she was pale. She looked familiar, like—

Cathleen's breath caught in her chest. It was the woman she'd seen earlier. The woman from the restaurant.

Cathleen stuttered something wordlike and half-stumbled to the door. Marty was standing by the window, studying a file when she spilled out of her office into his. He offered her half a glance before placing the file down and giving his bonsai tree a disinterested poke.

"What's the good word, toots?"

A dry squeak came out where her words should have been. Cathleen cleared her throat and tried again.

"Mm hmm." Marty wasn't listening. He grunted, fiddling with his oxygen canister, then spritzed some water onto the bonsai tree. "You think that man here to see you has anything to do with it?"

"I told Jacey not to—" Cathleen stopped. "I'm sorry, who?"

"Out there, in reception." Marty sprayed some water over his shoulder toward the door.

Cathleen followed the trail of water droplets with her eyes and found the man. Blue jeans and a faded black blazer, elbow pads. A professor? His salt-and-pepper hair was spiked by a pair of reading glasses shoved back from his forehead. "What the hell does he want, Marty?"

"How should I know? He said he'd wait till we were finished, but he wanted a chance to talk to you, if one turned up. Just don't give away all our secrets, eh?" What was supposed to be a wry laugh turned into a series of choked coughs.

Cathleen watched Marty dab away spittle with his handkerchief, then turned back to the man in the lobby. "This oughta be good."

The man looked up when Cathleen pushed open the main door to the office. It was typically noisy in the communal area, though today things were worse than usual with the grinding and pounding sounds coming from the construction down the hall. She offered a dry smile and took a seat across from him in one of the lobby chairs. *Jesus, these things are uncomfortable.*

"Cathleen Williams, I presume?"

"You presume correctly. And you are...?" She tried to keep her tone light, but the fact that she was a busy woman with more to do than anyone else in the building wafted off of her designer shoes and tailored jacket. And her head had just started to ache.

"Mrs. Willi—"

"'Ms.,' if you don't mind."

"Of course. Ms. Williams." He inhaled deeply and grinned. "Like the Ms. Dior you're wearing."

Cathleen leveled her gaze at him, taking him in from his eyeglass-spiked hair to his cheap wingtips. "Is that a come on?"

His smile flattened. "It seems you've had an interesting few days, *Ms. Williams.* Care to tell me about them?"

She did not have time for this. Not today. "I'm sure I don't know what you mean."

"I'm sure you don't." The man stretched and pulled his pants up around his waist, then drew a business card from his coat pocket. "But in case anything comes to mind about the last few days—anything strange you can recall...you just get ahold of me."

"Fine, fine. Thanks for the card. I have no idea what the hell you're talking about, but I have had a weird day, so yeah, maybe something will shake out. Oh, and the perfume is 'Miss.' *Miss* Dior." She looked at the card in her hand. "Enjoy your day, Detective Putnam."

"Yeah...sure thing." He took the glasses from the top of his head and slid them onto his face. Of course, then he had to look over them to study her. He gave her a long, hard look. "You sure you're feeling all right, Ms. Williams?"

Cathleen brushed her hair from her face with a huff. "I'm just fine, Detective. And I have a lot to do, so if you'd please..." She motioned toward the building's exit.

The man stared at her for another long moment, running his tongue along the inside of his cheek. He was thinking something, and he seemed to be laughing at some running joke she didn't get. She turned and walked toward her office, stopping momentarily to watch him amble away, whistling a tune, his hands stuffed in his pockets. Something about the man bothered her, deeply.

"Cathleen?"

The voice snapped her from her thoughts and an involuntary glare contorted her face. *Who the hell wanted what NOW?*

It was one of the scrubs from the medical facility they were putting in next door. A flour sack with a mop of curly hair. Only an idiot would have that hair. He was holding his stethoscope in the air like a surrender flag, approaching her like she was a rabid dog. How the hell did he know her name, anyway?

"It's Ms. Williams, thank you. What do you want? You're not interrupting my work enough with that incessant hammering over there? I thought you guys would be finished by now."

The pathetic little man shrank back a bit more with each sentence she spat out. Another man, this one in a white jacket, walked over and put a reassuring hand on the scrub's forearm, nodding silently. "I think that's enough, James. Why don't you let me speak to Ms. Williams?"

Cathleen was walking into her office by that point, grinding her teeth against the stabbing pain in her head. She had no time for any of this. The whole day was gone, it seemed, and she'd only had blown interviews by too-tight skirts. She still needed to finish that damned insurance policy Marty was hounding her about.

Another lightning strike to the temple. She let go of the door and grabbed the sides of her head. The man in the white coat was at her side, immediately.

"Ms. Williams, please. Sit." He led her to one of the lobby chairs. "You've been through a lot today."

Cathleen let him sit next to her while she caught her breath. The stabbing in her temple hadn't gone away, but she had found its rhythm. "I'm sorry...do I know you?"

"I'm Doctor Thomas. We met this morning. Do you remember our conversation?"

She tried to look him in the eye, study his face. His eyes were a twinkly green. Did she recognize him? He had a salt and pepper beard and receding hairline. When was this morning? The room blurred and the sound of his voice rose to an echo. "Cathleen? Can you hear me?"

The only sound she heard was the plastic clatter of her phone when she hit the floor.

***

It took a few blinks for things to come into focus, and even then, Cathleen was only aware of her throbbing skull. It looked like she was in her bedroom, at least. What day was it, Wednesday? She had been drinking pretty hard lately, though it had been a long time since she'd blacked out on a weeknight.

Someone started hammering next door and Cathleen threw the pillow over her head to protect her aching temples. *Who the hell is hammering at—oh, shit. What time is it?*

She threw an arm out from under the covers and pawed at the nightstand. Eventually she followed the charging cord to where the phone had landed behind the bed. *At least I plugged it in*, she thought. Then her eyes bugged out when she saw it was nine in the morning. She hadn't been late in six years.

Part of her wanted to spring out of bed and make the coffee-spilling, mad dash for the office. That's what they always did on TV and movies when the hungover main character was late. Cathleen knew herself. The mad dash didn't suit her.

She pressed a few buttons on her phone then held it to her ear. "Yeah, Marty? Uh huh…I know, can you believe it? Yeah, I'm a mess over here. I'll stay at the home office today…yup, I'll email them over in time for your two o'clock. Right. All right, see you tomorrow."

The hammering was right above her bed on the other side of the wall. She gave the wall a few kicks before rolling out of bed for a shower and some aspirin.

It was going to be an easy day, Cathleen told herself. After those interviews yesterday…were they really that bad? She had blacked out not long after. Something must have gotten her going, if she was that far gone on a Tuesday afternoon. She wasn't a drunk by business standards, but she would be if she didn't dial it back. Maybe she'd go for a run later.

Coffee in hand, she snuggled down in front of the computer to send some emails, check a few documents, then hit snooze on that new project. The truth was, Marty hadn't been doing so well these last few years, and the numbers at the office had been suffering as a result. There was an audit coming up and so she might as well get a relaxing day in while she still could. And he wouldn't stop bugging her about the insurance updates.

A stab of pain seared through her temples. *Damn it,* she thought. *Why did I remind myself of the insurance bullshit?* She punched a few keys on the laptop, then wiggled the mouse. *And why isn't this loading?* After a couple of restarts and a few dozen clicks, she realized the wi-fi was down. A power drill groaning through the walls was all she needed. She picked up her keys, shouldered her laptop bag, and walked out of the apartment.

Ten years ago, she might have powered through her headache and gone for a run. Not today. She had no one to impress. Her laptop bag kept her from bothering with a jog and besides, she was comfortable enough in her own skin to put running in the "Things Not Going to Happen Today" column.

Everything in her life ran in columns and tables. There was a file for each thought, idea, project; a deadline and a budget. This was how she operated. It was the only way to get things done.

Cathleen didn't feel the need to impress anyone, but she could also hear her doctor's voice chiding her that if she couldn't fit in a run, she could at least try some brisk walking.

A face flashed in her mind, a man with green eyes and a beard, wearing a white coat. Doctor...?

She worked through her memory while she walked, trying to put a name with the face. A hot lance pierced through her skull then, and she doubled over from the pain. *This is no ordinary headache*, she thought to herself.

She took a seat on the stoop of an antique store to catch her breath. It was closed for remodeling so at least she wouldn't be in anyone's way. But remodel meant more hammering and drilling, and Cathleen found herself stomping away from yet another construction site. *Seriously, what the hell?*

Just a coffee, that's all she needed, and she was almost there. Up ahead, she saw a bulldozer and a front loader in the coffeeshop's parking lot. Cathleen figured she'd try to set up her laptop at the cafe but was already mentally preparing to hike to the library instead. She sighed. The whole goddamn city couldn't be under construction.

Cathleen waited at the intersection for the light to turn. The coffee house was just across the street. Waiting beside her, a few students tapped their thumbs on the screens of their phones, and a homeless woman sat despondent at their feet, her cardboard sign propped up against her knees.

Got Fired. Spare Change Appreciated, it read. The woman held out a cup with a shaking hand. Cathleen's lip curled reflexively, and she thought to herself that it was no surprise the woman had been fired. She could hardly hold a cup. What use could she be? Then Cathleen's eyes traveled from the greasy cardboard sign to the shaking hand to the woman's face.

She dropped her laptop bag and took a step backward. It was the woman she'd bumped into at McDonald's yesterday morning, and again at the interview, somehow. But her face...her face was gone wrong. It had been singed horribly on the one side, and blackened skin flaked at the edges of red, exposed muscle and a row of naked teeth. Something like what came from a hot glue gun oozed from the woman's left eye, straight out of the pupil. The words on her sign had changed, too: *Burned by Fire. Hardly a Scratch.*

Seeing Cathleen's reaction, the woman's mangled face broke into a grin. "Spare change?"

Cathleen tried to turn; her plan was simply to run—fast, and far away. Instead, the heel of her shoe caught in the strap of the laptop bag she'd dropped. She tripped sideways, tumbling directly into the traffic streaming by. One of the college students screamed and Cathleen heard a car horn somewhere off in the distance.

All of the sounds were drowned out, though, by the sound of the homeless woman laughing, shrieking, choking on her words *"Spare change?"* and then falling into her mindless cackle once again.

***

Cathleen wasn't sure if it was the beeping or the roar of the power drill that woke her up. She was in a hospital bed. Jesus, she must have hit the sidewalk harder than she'd thought. That stupid old store manager. How many times had Cathleen warned her she needed to salt the sidewalk in front of the store?

"Ah, look who's awake!" A young man in green scrubs walked into the room and made a beeline for her IV. He had curly brown hair and a pudgy, sweet-looking face. Not unlike a hobbit, she supposed. "How's the head, Ms. Williams?"

Cathleen frowned. "Now that you mention it, though— yeah. My head is pounding. What is that, power of suggestion?"

"No suggesting at all. You're pretty severely concussed, Ms. Williams." The young man had her follow his pen light, then his finger. "Do you remember how you got here?"

"Well yeah, it was that stupid dope at the corner store. Her gutters drain right onto the sidewalk and when they freeze— what? What's that look for?"

He gave a noncommittal shrug. "Sorry. Didn't realize I was looking any way. So, you slipped on the ice, then?"

"Yeah, and I'm pretty sure I want to file a suit. I mean, I *warned* her about that stupid sidewalk!"

The young man folded his arms and stared at her intently. "Sidewalk? Not stairs?"

"Yeah. Right in front of her store." Cathleen frowned at him. "Why are you looking at me like that? What stairs?"

Another voice interrupted their conversation. "Is everything all right, Ms. Williams?" A balding man wearing a white coat over his scrubs had entered the room. He peered over the top of a chart, studying her.

At the sight of him, Cathleen felt a stab of pain in her temple. He looked familiar. "Ow," she breathed. "No, not all right. My head is killing me."

"Yes, the headache is a concern. We want to get you back to feeling better. Doctor Fortin here has arranged for you to have a CAT scan later today. Can you tell me what you remem—" The grinding whine of a power drill cut him off.

"God DAMN it! What is wrong with you people?"

The man in the white coat ignored her outburst. He took a pen light from his pocket and shined it in her eye. She slapped it away. "Get that stupid thing away from me! Doctor Frodo over here already shined his flashlight in my face. My head hurts and no one is making me feel *better!* It's all flashlights and construction!"

"My dear, I'm so sorry." The older doctor exchanged a look with the younger.

"You don't seem sorry. Isn't it a bit ridiculous to have construction going on where there are patients trying to recover? It's goddamn cruel!" She gripped the hair on the sides of her head. "My head is *killing* me!"

The older doctor paused for a moment, studying her, then wiped his nose with a handkerchief. "I quite agree. Construction zones and hospitals don't mix. But you're quite a special case. There wasn't really anywhere else to put you. For now, at least. No matter. Doctor Fortin will administer some pain medication to help you sleep."

Doctor Fortin followed him into the hallway. Cathleen did her best to eavesdrop on the conversation they had at the nurse's station across the hall, but the construction sounds chopped up their words. Still, she managed to piece together something about falling down an elevator shaft, a car accident, slipping on ice. The older doctor's droning voice cut through the construction. "…It's something different every day…"

Sounds like a busy patient roster, she thought. *God, my head is killing me.*

Doctor Fortin came back in, a small syringe in his hand. "Ms. Williams, this is going to help you sleep. I'll be back this afternoon to take you in for your scan." He tinkered with her IV while he spoke. "Sweet dreams."

***

It must have been Jackson's clipboard smacking down on the table that jarred Cathleen awake. No one seemed to notice she'd dozed off. Too many long days this month. It was starting to catch up to her. Then again, another board meeting? Even on her best day she would have slept through it. Besides, Jackson and the other grunts could shoulder some of the weight for once.

C-Click. C-Click.

Cathleen glared in the office manager's direction. Floppy blonde hair with an arrogant smile, Jackson always brought a pen that he wouldn't stop clicking. She was up to her ears in renewing the office insurance policy and could hardly keep up with prepping for the audit on top of that, and all she could think about was the irregular rhythm of his pen. *C-c-click. Click. C-click.*

Down the conference room table, none of them did anything to make Cathleen's job easier. All they had to contribute was noise. Knuckles on the table, whining chairs, shuffling feet, cleared nasal passages.

Marty was hashing out some details on a subparagraph of the mission statement, opening another piece of candy. It squeaked and crinkled as he twisted the metallic paper. Wasn't he supposed to be in for another round of treatments? The old man leaned over to review the notes Jackson had taken down, his oxygen machine clicking and whistling as he breathed. That goddamn pen wouldn't let up, either. Cathleen squeezed her eyes shut to block out the noise, as if that would work. *Stupid, Cathleen. Stupid!*

Then a rhythmic whirring grew louder, the vacuum cleaner edging its way up the hallway. It didn't help things. Esther must be working early tonight—or was the board meeting just running late? Cathleen checked her watch. 9:17. *Jesus, Marty.*

She stood up and made her way to the door. Maybe some more coffee was in order if the old man was going to have her running more quotes once he'd finished up with Jackson.

Cathleen nodded a greeting at the cleaning lady as she passed her in the hallway. The older woman couldn't hear a damn thing anyone said, vacuum or no. And apparently having the top executives meeting in the conference room didn't deter her from shutting down and cleaning out the coffee machine.

Son of a bitch, Cathleen muttered to herself. She turned on her heel to head back to the meeting and slipped on the break room's linoleum instead, hitting her elbow on the "wet floor" sign on the way down.

"Miss Cathleen!" Esther called over the sweeper. She ran over to Cathleen, crouching beside her. "Are you all right?"

Cathleen rubbed her insulted elbow and jerked away from Esther. Just what she needed, that derelict woman breathing on her. "Yes, Esther, I'm fine. Other than my wounded pride." The vacuum whirred in a blaring white panel of noise. Esther hadn't turned it off.

Marty peeked his head out from the conference room and hurried over when he saw the two women sitting on the ground. His oxygen tank clattered behind him.

Esther looked like she would cry. "Oh, Miss Cathleen, I am so sorry! I didn't mean for anyone to get hurt. I should have waited until you were all out of the building—"

He held out his hand to the older woman to help her to her feet. "None of that, Esther." He grinned and pointed. "See look, the wet floor sign is up and everything. Nothing to mark down on an insurance form, eh Cathleen? No harm done." His oxygen tank clicked and whistled under the broad hum of the vacuum.

Cathleen was eyeing her shirt, noting the small white blotches showing up on the fabric. She sniffed at her sleeve. There must have been some bleach mixed in with the mop water. Mixed with her Miss Dior perfume, it was nauseating. *Son of a bitch, this was a nice shirt.* She gave him a glare but accepted his outstretched hand. "My hero," she said, rolling her eyes.

Marty let out one of his belly laughs, too loud for the occasion, and patted her on the back. "Oh, Cathleen. You are the best." He turned to share the laugh with Esther, but found the cleaning lady wringing her hands, practically falling over again. "That's enough of that, young lady! Don't worry about Cathleen, she's cranky by nature. I mean, hell, she'd complain if you hit her with a new car." He laughed at his own joke, and his oxygen tank rattled and hissed in errant harmony with the vacuum.

Cathleen wheeled on Esther and spat, "Would you *please* turn off that sweeper?"

Esther jumped visibly and clambered toward her vacuum cleaner. The empty space the lack of sound made was louder than the space it had filled. Cathleen's temples throbbed.

Marty exhaled loudly, satisfied. Always the smug satisfaction. "There now, isn't that better? And look at Cathleen, here." He grinned. "Hardly a scratch."

Cathleen punched the wall, upsetting the framed posters hanging there. "Hardly a scratch? Hardly…a *scratch?* This is a three-hundred-dollar shirt that I'll never wear again! God *damn* it, Marty! I need to get out of here."

On her way back to the conference room she heard Marty speaking softly with Esther, followed by the tell-tale crinkle of a toffee candy as he gave one to the bewildered woman, who really did look like she might throw up or pass out. Cathleen knew he wouldn't get back to work until he'd sufficiently consoled her. As ruthless as he was, the man couldn't resist a vulnerable woman.

***

Cathleen packed up to leave. She wasn't going to get much done stinking like bleach, especially not with Esther's sniveling noises added to the office mix. In the hopes she might get something done after her head cleared, she threw the files she needed into a box to take home. She scrunched her lips and threw her glare out the office window when she heard the familiar click and whistle coming down the hall.

"I thought I might find you sneaking away."

He leaned on the doorway, loosening his tie. He was trying to catch his breath without being obvious about it, but she knew.

"Yeah, Mart. It's been a hell of a day. And I'm just about finished—"

"Honestly…" Marty put up a hand to stop her. "I know you'll get it done. You always do. It's why I like having you around."

Cathleen smiled. God, he could deflate her. She hated that he could make her smile when she was so angry. "The tight ass doesn't hurt either, though, does it?"

He responded with a wheezy chuckle and then stepped into the office, shutting the door behind him. "You've been with me since the very beginning, toots. When we were still working out of a broom closet. Hard to imagine we'd be pulling a two-million-dollar policy on these digs, huh?" He eyeballed the walls and ceiling as he spoke.

It had been what, seventeen years? Twice they very nearly shut down. This latest was just a small scare, and a few well-timed settlements would keep them afloat. But it wasn't like Marty to wax sentimental. And why now, when all she wanted to do was get in the tub?

"What I'm trying to say is, I know I can count on your loyalty. Right, Cathleen?"

There it was. He wasn't being sentimental. She met the old man's eyes and they were focused, blazing cobalt. The only sound was the click and hiss of the oxygen.

"Marty, what—?"

"Things aren't going well. You have to know it."

"Oh, but the Bickford settlement is going to help, and—"

"It's more than just the overhead. Cathleen, I've gotten into…some trouble. I…" he trailed off.

"Marty, what is it?" Cathleen set her things down and gave him a hard stare. "C'mon, there's nothing we haven't dealt with before. We survived 2008, didn't we?"

The old man gave a wheezy exhale that might have been a laugh, but he was shaking his head. "There's more to it than that. Really, the less you know on that end, the better. The fact is, I'm going to need to ask for your help if any of us want to keep our retirement." He coughed a phlegmy cough. "Or stay out of prison."

***

The streetlights made stripes of light in the car as Cathleen rode home. She'd been biking to and from the office lately, but given the long day and the atom bomb Marty had dropped on her at the end of it, she opted for the cab.

He was going to torch the place. Wait till everyone was out of the building, and boom. But he couldn't do it, not on his own.

He tried to blame it on the oxygen, saying, "I just can't move fast enough, Cathleen," but the both of them knew that wasn't it. He didn't lack the speed, he lacked the cunning.

Cathleen and Marty both knew the reason they'd stayed afloat as long as they had was because of her creative thinking. So here it was, the ultimate test. And it wasn't just loyalty. If they couldn't recover some of their losses through the insurance, Cathleen was likely to lose it all.

Son of a bitch, Marty.

It was going to be a double Ambien evening, looked like. There was too much work to do and too much worrying, but it would have to wait until the next day. She was going to need her strength.

***

"Rise and shine, pumpkin pie."

Cathleen's eyes snapped open at the sound of a strange voice in her room. When she looked around her, she was even more bewildered. She'd fallen asleep in her bedroom, but here she was in a hospital gown, lying in a hospital room. The machine next to her beeped and she could hear construction pounding away down the hall.

She looked for where the voice had come from. A dark-haired man was grinning at her, seated close to her on the bed. Too close. *Who the hell*—then she remembered. She'd met him before. It was that smarmy detective. What was his name again? Putnam.

Holy hell, her head hurt. Each beep out of the machine bounced around the inside of her skull.

"What the—why are you here? Why am *I* here? Isn't this a private—" Cathleen's thoughts whirled into a fury until she stopped herself. *Focus, Cathleen.* Questions later. She wanted this man removed immediately. "*Hello?* Somebody help me, please!"

An orderly came in and stopped short, looking from the detective to Cathleen. "Yes, Miss Williams?"

Another man was right on his heels, the doctor in green scrubs...the hobbit-looking one, Doctor Fortin. When he spoke to her, his voice was cold. "What seems to be the problem, Cathleen?"

She rubbed her temples, trying to ease the throbbing and clear her head. *Who the hell were these people and why did she know them?*

Detective Putnam spoke up. "There's no problem, Doc. Just paying a visit and taking a precaution, is all." He took Cathleen's wrist and gently pulled it away from her face.

"Don't you touch me!" Cathleen spat at him. She used her free arm to land a few slaps against his arms, trying to push him away.

"Easy now, easy. I don't want to add 'assaulting an officer.'" He latched her wrist to her bed with a pair of handcuffs.

The orderly and Doctor Fortin had rushed forward to restrain their patient, but Cathleen fell back against the pillows when she felt the handcuffs. She stared at the detective in a daze. "I—I'm sorry. I don't understand . . ."

"Really, sir, is this necessary?" the orderly looked from the doctor to the detective, flustered.

Detective Putnam snorted. "Someone was trying to pay our esteemed executive a visit in the office... before the whole thing went *kapow*." He held up a square glass bottle with a metal bow at the top. Cathleen squinted with vague recollection. It was her perfume bottle.

"Where did you...? That was in my desk."

"No, not anymore. You've got a cleaning lady with sticky fingers. They found it on her when she was admitted. After she told me you'd rigged the place." He opened the bottle and spritzed some into the air, then grinned. On his way out of the room, he stopped by the doctor. "I'd say our little arsonist here could use some extra supervision."

***

The sound of her breathing woke her, a ragged pant. She squinted from side to side, instinctively looking for a light source, but she couldn't see a thing. Were her eyes even open? It was too dark for anything to register. And then the pain came creeping, tiptoeing around from the back of her ears to the sides and front of her skull. The first throb landed like a blunt object.

What the hell happened?

Lights were blaring across her field of vision now, shattering the dark into shards. There was yelling. Footsteps, tromping boots running past her.

"Ma'am. Ma'am? Can you hear me?"

Cathleen let out a croak and the blunt object smashed against her skull again. *Jesus God, it hurts.* "Yes...yes. I'm here..."

But the man hadn't been speaking to Cathleen. Another voice answered, this one more clearly than she'd been able to. "I'm okay, sir. You see to that lady over there."

Esther.

It was Esther's voice.

Cathleen managed to open her eyes, finally, squinting against the lights. Emergency vehicles, everywhere. She saw the man make a gesture to another group of paramedics, who came running to the spot holding a stretcher.

"You just stay still, ma'am. These guys are going to get you help. Don't move. You hear me?"

"I'm just f-fine, sir…" Esther said.

He didn't respond to the older woman, or even hear her. He was already running off toward the flaming structure. Esther's eyes landed on Cathleen's, and her singed face wrinkled. Was it a smile? A glare? Her voice came out as a choked rasp.

"Hardly a—hardly a scratch."

Cathleen let out a groan and rolled to her back. The flaming structure in front of her was the building she'd worked in for nearly twenty years; the building she'd just torched. A little tinkering with the gas and a well-timed spark from the microwave in the staff kitchen. Too easy.

Flames licked out of the faux-Victorian windowsills, wafting heat into the black sky. A team of emergency workers leaned over Esther, working gently and quickly to get her onto a stretcher.

The EMTs waved off a group of police officers wanting to ask questions, but Cathleen watched as a grumpy-looking man in a cheap suit sidled up to Esther. The old woman's voice was like an old frog's as she spoke with him. Cathleen couldn't make out the words. The man gestured toward the building, standing lonely behind a wall of flames.

No one was supposed to be in the building. *Goddammit, Esther.*

As if she'd heard Cathleen's thoughts, the old cleaning woman moved her head slowly to the side and met Cathleen's eyes. A soot-stained finger rose up and pointed directly at her.

Cathleen's stomach went cold and panic rose up into her throat, ejecting onto the concrete as a load of bile. The man pulled a pad of paper from his pocket and began walking toward her.

***

"I'm so sorry! I didn't mean to frighten you, Miss Williams."

Cathleen had nearly shrieked when she heard Esther's voice. No one was supposed to be here. No one.

The old woman was trembling. "I hoped to catch you—I-I just wanted to...to tell you again how bad I felt about your blouse.

"Oh, Christ, Esther." Cathleen reminded herself to smile. The woman already looked like she might melt straight into the floor. "Remember? Hardly a scratch." Cathleen put her hand on Esther's back, leading her away from the break room, away from the timer on the microwave.

"I-I know it's not as fancy as the clothes you usually wear, Miss Williams, but I hoped m-maybe you could find yourself something nice with this coupon. I felt so bad about the bleach on your blouse." Esther had stopped in the hallway and pulled a crinkled coupon from her pocket.

Cathleen took the paper and looked down at it. There was a JCPenney logo on it. *Oh, hell.* She fought to keep her lip from curling in disgust. Trying to fix the problem, the old lady had insulted her more than anything else. And then Cathleen caught a hint of a familiar scent coming from the paper. It was her own perfume. Cathleen looked hard at Esther. Had she...?

This was not the time or place to worry about theft. How long had Esther been there, and what had she seen? Why was she even in the building?

It didn't matter. They needed to get out of there. "It's late, Esther, and everyone in the building is gone. This couldn't have waited?"

The woman looked down at her hands, her face flushed. "I'm so sorry, Ms. Williams. I-I was going to leave it in your mailbox but then I saw you walking in. I—well, I just followed you." She squirmed underneath Cathleen's hard stare. Finally, she shrugged and tried to sound breezy with a higher-pitched voice. "Working late again?"

Cathleen's mouth broke into a forced grin. "You got it, Esther. All kinds of paperwork to fill out. Audits really are a bitch." She put a firm hand on the cleaning woman's shoulder, walking her down the hall. "It's been a long day, Esther. We need to get out of here if we know what's good for us."

***

The jangle of the handcuffs against the bed's metal railing startled Cathleen, but at least she remembered where she was.

A whining drill cut through her thoughts and confirmed her memory.

The hospital. She was safe. Aside from the same stupid headache she'd had for what, a week now? She couldn't have been in the hospital for that long. She'd gone home, hadn't she, and to work…she'd been going about her business like nothing had happened.

But something had happened. She'd done something terrible. Her brain ran in circles chasing the thought, trying to peg down what she was missing. That's when she heard the familiar click and whistle.

"You in there, Cathleen?"

God damn it, Marty.

"What are you doing here, Marty?" Her words came out as a hiss.

"Aw, c'mon now! Of course I'm here!"

"What the hell time is it?" The darkness bewildered her. Just as she said these words, a razor-sharp beam of light jolted the room awake. Marty was grinning in front of the blinds, having just ripped them open.

"Damn things must be industrial grade for blocking out light," she muttered.

"It's been a hell of a few days, Cathleen." *Click. Whistle.*

She waited for him to say more, to explain what was going on, but he just sat there, squinting and grinning at her.

Click. "They're going to burn us to the ground, you know." *Whistle.*

Cathleen grunted and tried to shift her weight in the bed. The handcuff clanged against the railing. "Marty. What the hell is going on?"

"What do you remember, toots?"

The darkness creeped in again at the edge of her vision. Something was scurrying into the dark corners in her mind, trying to get away. "I don't know, Marty. I don't understand what's happening. I'm going in circles and I keep waking up here." She raised her voice with each sentence to drown out the hammering noises coming from down the hall.

"Yeah." Marty cleared his throat and rubbed his knees. "The doctors can't tell me much, but they did let me know you're not real clear on how you ended up in here. That true? Can you remember anything, Cathleen?"

She twisted in the bed a bit. She was in the hospital because she had a concussion. The concussion was from...she'd fallen

on the ice in front of—no, that wasn't it. Was it an elevator
shaft? A car crash?

"Cathleen..." Marty's voice was thick. "Cathleen, honey.
They're just keeping you for observation because, well,
because they're worried about you." His words shook as they
fell from his mouth. Cathleen couldn't wrap her head around
them. "Something about trauma...the doctors are saying there's
nothing wrong with you, not a scratch on—"

"That's *it*." Cathleen's words came out as a hiss. "Not a
scratch, hardly a scratch—it was *Esther*. She's been following
me, harassing me. What's she want with me? Still pissed I
walked on her wet floor?"

"Sweetie." Marty squeezed his eyes closed and pinched the
bridge of his nose. "I don't suppose you remember talking to
me...before."

"Before what?" Cathleen squinted at him, studying his face.
Her head was starting to hurt again. Faint alarm bells were
coming at her from the sides of her mind.

"Just...before. Before now. Do you remember having this
conversation?"

"I don't understand what the hell you're talking about, Mart.
Just tell me what you're trying to say."

"Cleaning lady was walking out of the building with you
when it blasted. You know, Esther. She was tore up pretty bad.
Landed hard on the concrete and smashed herself up. She
uh...shit, Cathleen. Esther died last night."

Cathleen blinked a few times as his words landed, each one
like a raindrop in a pile of ash. Her thoughts spilled out every
which way but she kept shaking her head, back and forth, back
and forth. He wasn't making sense. They must have changed
his medicine. Esther wasn't dead. She'd walked out of the

building…Cathleen clanged her handcuffed wrist against the metal railing. "What the *hell* are you saying, Marty? This doesn't make any sense."

Marty shook his head and leaned in closer to her. He smelled like one of those stupid toffees. "Cathleen, you rigged up the office. I don't know what the hell made you do it. Gas and everything. Esther was there, too. Says she saw you in there." His face was right by hers. "She talked to that sumbitch detective right before she—Jesus, Cathleen. You don't remember anything?"

The machines answered for her, the beeps and tones swirling into a frenzy and joining mid-twirl with the roar of a jackhammer. The concerned look on the night nurse's face was the last thing Cathleen saw.

***

This dark, it was different. It was deeper than ink. This dark was sinister. *This dark has legs*. It tugged at the corners of her eyes when she turned her head. Something fearful scurried against the walls, something that didn't want to be seen. Something she didn't want to see.

Holy hell, I've got to stop drinking with the Ambien.

Cathleen rolled from her bed and shuffled about in her usual morning blur, preparing for the day. Once she'd dressed and put on her face, she spritzed some Miss Dior on her wrists.

She'd have to leave early again because Marty was really on a kick for those greasy breakfast sliders. They'd be the death of him, for sure. And goddammit, no doubt he was going to stick her with those interviews today.

The Cardboard Box

The familiar bell jingled as the door clanged shut. The smell of stale cigar smoke and dust welcomed her, and the man sitting with his newspaper spread across the counter looked up and smiled.

"Long time, little missie!"

The woman nodded, her stringy dark hair streaked across her featureless face. It was the sort of face that didn't register, but the man had known her a long time. Esther had been a customer when his wife Judy ran things. "Hi, Gene." Her voice was a murmur. "It's good to be back."

High Street Antiques was a place for curiosities and consignments, located just off the main drag of a forgettable but inimitable midwestern small town business district. Its rooms were labyrinthian; the spiral staircases and corridors lined with trinkets, furniture, fabrics, and jewelry.

It was one of Esther's favorite places. She stopped in every few months, fading into one hallway and emerging from a room somewhere on the upper level an hour later, never making a sound.

Once, Judy had nearly locked up and gone home for the night before realizing Esther was still in the store. "I'd just curl up and sleep right there," Esther had said, indicating a lustrous green couch draped with paisleyed velvet.

Judy donned her coat and gestured for Esther to follow her out the door. "It's too busy here. Home base is a bit

131

more…stark—if I can keep Gene from bringing home more of the store!"

"Good shelving helps," Esther had said.

Judy tsked. "Don't I know it. Fancy a look at some new units?"

Esther passed, that time.

Later, when Judy's cancer finally took her, Esther tidied their home for the funeral proceedings. She gathered the dust into an old vase she'd found with Judy's things and dropped it carefully into her pocket before giving Gene a farewell hug. He had thanked her for her help, wiping an eye when he turned away.

On the occasions when she needed to accommodate her expanding collection, Esther would take home a new curio cabinet. Today was different.

"I need something special today, Gene."

The old man snapped the newspaper, using it to hide his smile. "I know the feeling. Another holy grail, I suspect?"

"Something like that."

The thing she was after was still where she'd hidden it her previous visit. Gene didn't rearrange the inventory often, and she knew it'd be safe under the table of votives.

"Found it already?" Gene groaned as he stood up, making his way to the register. "Sorry. You're quick today."

Esther approached with an understanding smile, treasure in hand. "I've had my eye on this for a while." She set the item down. It was a tin canister for Charles Chips.

When she'd first seen it, over a year ago, it knocked the wind out of her. The cigarette-stain yellow of the container and its brown letters transported her to her father's knee, where he'd hugged her close and they'd shared handfuls of crispy chips.

He'd said to her in a sad sort of way, "I've got to get all my snuggles in. Before long you'll be too old and too big to sit on my lap. The world isn't ready for you, Esther."

The tin was only five dollars but it had taken more currency than that for Esther to work up the nerve to take the thing home. Gene counted her money and waved amiably as the door chime cheered their transaction.

Esther let the canister sit on her kitchen counter for a long while before she attended to it. She took careful steps around the room, the seconds on the clock timing her movements like a metronome. There were 3,500 seconds in an hour. She'd counted, more than once, in her private mausoleum.

Motion shook the dust, even imperceptibly, and she was a curator of dust. The vials and urns before her were a testament to the turn her life had taken. No one visited. Her mother, her sister…there was no way she could explain.

Esther stood before her shelves, examining her trinkets as people did their books. Each container had its story.

Opening a cupboard at the base of one of the shelving units, Esther removed a shabby cardboard box. Of all the things she'd taken, over the years, this was the only item she felt was theft. Her mother had never noticed. At least, she never spoke of it.

Esther was not yet in junior high the day her dad didn't make it home. In the following days, strangers filled the house, and Esther receded into the background. Then came the box.

"It's just his ashes," her mother had said. "Ashes don't matter. His spirit is with God, now."

Esther opened the box and laid her open palm across its soft, powdered insides. These were his fingers, his hands that pushed her on the swing, the legs that walked with her to school. This box held him, as he had held her.

For years, she'd hidden it away. She couldn't look at the box without feeling his eyes on her, his arms squeezing her, her fat little finger tracing his stubbly chin. He'd hug her on his lap, and she was safe. She was real.

His lap, where he'd held her, had disappeared before she outgrew it. Those were old memories; they were ash. There was nothing but death in that box. No new dust.

Esther had worked hard to collect new memories of him, pressing her mother and sister, her aunt and cousins, anyone, for odd little tidbits or things they missed most. But it hurt to talk about and it wasn't long before her questions were met with sulky stares.

They avoided her, left the room when she entered. It was somehow easier that way. And if she kept things tidy and neat, they wouldn't find her.

Lifting the cardboard box, Esther tipped its contents into the chips canister, and a thirty-year-old sob caught in her throat.

Acknowledgements

I am grateful to all of the people who asked me when I was going to write a book. You just read it. I hope I did not disappoint.

I am grateful to all of those who have cleaned with me in the course of my life, and those yet to come. Seriously. Do the dishes. I'm grateful. Others will be, too. You don't have to bottle up the suds or put the ashes in a container, or anything like that. In fact, I don't recommend it. That was fiction.

In real life, clean up whether or not you'll end up on an acknowledgements page. Put the bowl in the sink—better yet, put it in the dishwasher or just wash it yourself. Do the people cleaning up after you get paid enough for you to not rinse out your oatmeal bowl? No, they don't. No one does. And while you're at it, the laundry probably needs to be switched.

About the Author

Leah McNaughton Lederman is a writer and freelance editor from the Indianapolis area, where she lives with her husband and an assortment of children, cats, and dogs. She is the creator and editor of *Café Macabre: A Collection of Horror Short Stories and Art by Women*, released by SourcePoint Press. Leah's short stories and poems have appeared in Scout Media's *A Matter of Words, A Contract of Words*, Clarendon House's *Fireburst* and *Cadence*, and Indie Author's Press *Issues of Tomorrow: A Sci-fi Anthology*. Follow her on Facebook at www.facebook.com/ledermanediting, on Twitter @leahlederman, and sign up for her newsletter at http://ccpurl.com/gJMwa1 .

Made in the USA
San Bernardino, CA
22 February 2020